Dust Devils

Western Literature Series

Books by Robert Laxalt

The Violent Land: Tales the Old Timers Tell

Sweet Promised Land

A Man in the Wheatfield

Nevada

In a Hundred Graves: A Basque Portrait

Nevada: A Bicentennial History

A Cup of Tea in Pamplona

The Basque Hotel

A Time We Knew: Images of Yesterday
in the Basque Homeland

Child of the Holy Ghost

A Lean Year and Other Stories

The Governor's Mansion

Dust Devils

Dust Devils

Robert Laxalt

University of Nevada Press

Reno   Las Vegas

Western Literature Series

University of Nevada Press, Reno, Nevada 89557 USA

Copyright © 1997 by Robert Laxalt

Manufactured in the United States of America

Book design by Carrie Nelson House

Library of Congress Cataloging-in-Publication Data

Laxalt, Robert, 1923–

Dust devils / Robert Laxalt.

p. cm.

ISBN 0-87417-300-0 (paper ed.)

I. Title.

PS3562.A9525D8 1997   97-15224

813'.54—dc21   CIP

The paper used in this book meets the requirements of American

National Standard for Information Sciences—Permanence of Paper

or Printed Library Materials, ANSI Z39.48–1984. Binding

materials were selected for strength and durability.

06 05 04 03 02 01 00 99 98   5 4 3

for Tom Radko

Dust Devils

Riding at an easy walk beside his father's big roan, Ira wondered who was going to give way when white man and Indian reached the point of convergence on the wagon road.

That they would converge at just about the same time and place, there was little doubt. The Indian cavalcade had been climbing the trail from the bottom of the canyon for at least an hour. It was an unhurried climb on the hairline trail through the soft gray clumps of rabbit brush.

Black Rock Tom on his pinto stallion would not make a show of hurrying any more than Ira's father would. It was beneath his dignity. Ira reflected on how similar the two men were, though that was a comparison he would never dare make in his father's presence.

Even their faces resembled each other if one forgot about the coloring. Their features might have been sculpted out of the same stone, the only difference being that Black Rock Tom seemed always to be scowling and Ira's father, John D. Hamilton by God, looked and was stubborn.

Black Rock Tom's band was keeping to the old way of traveling single file on the thin trail, a holdover from the time when braves under attack could wheel and dash off in many directions instead of one, unlike the white man's posse who traveled shoulder to shoulder three and even four abreast, making a confused mess of scattering when they were attacked. Actually, there was no need for that fighting order of riding nowadays, nor had there been for twenty years and more. Still, memories were long and tempers short if trouble were to flare. One look at the heavy rifle tucked into its worn scabbard under his father's stirrup fender said nearly all there was to say about being ready for trouble the instant it came. That and his father's dictum that to go un-armed in Indian country even now was a good way to sepa-rate yourself from your scalp lock.

What a pretty sight the Paiutes made when they were mov-ing camp, Ira thought as he looked down upon the winding ribbon of color—red, yellow, green, blue, and even black. That was another sentiment that could never be voiced be-tween father and son. Anything Indian seemed to be for-bidden ground. Ira's friendship with Cricket, Black Rock Tom's son, was the exception, and that was because Cricket had been Ira's only playmate since as far back as when he took his first step.

That in turn was because Cricket's mother had taken the place of Ira's mother in all ways after his blood mother had died in childbirth. That was the price one paid for living a distance from white neighbors. Ira had lived part of that year in Black Rock Tom's wickiup with his wife and Cricket. The wickiup was cone-shaped and protected on the outside by long rushes of tules tied together and bound in layers to the lodge poles. Bearskin rugs covered the floor, and a smoke hole at the apex of the lodge poles drew both flame and smoke upwards and out.

"Letting you suckle Indian was my first and biggest mistake," John D. Hamilton by God had said to Ira so many times that the meaning had been lost on the boy. The same went for Black Rock Tom. His endless repetition was, "The only presents white man gave us was gunpowder, whiskey, and smallpox." The words had long ago gone unheard by Ira. Riding at the head of his cavalcade, Black Rock Tom was decked out in all his finery. So were his men, once called braves but just Injuns now, who followed behind him. Indians loved white-man parades, and the Fourth of July parade in Sierraville was the "biggest and wildest of them all" in that isolated pocket of northeastern California.

Compared to Sacramento to the west and Virginia City in neighboring Nevada, Sierraville wasn't much as far as towns went, but it was the best Heavenly Valley had to offer. It could boast fourteen buildings, and that was saying some.

There was a certain reasoning that ordered the makeup of the town. The wide dirt street that would not know paving for a long time to come was bounded at one end by a church with a steeple, a schoolhouse, and the Grange hall for town meetings and dances-at-any-excuse. The schoolhouse was classroom to six girls and four boys, and contained a pot-bellied stove for winter. A stage in the Grange hall served as podium for speakers, a permanent piano too heavy to move at will, and space enough for a drummer, banjo and fiddle players, and brass instrumentalists. Whenever there was a dance, the long wooden benches for community affairs were moved over to the walls to provide seating for the old and infirm, wallflower maidens, and children

3

who preferred the noise of music and stomping feet to the relative quiet of the sleeping loft where they could spread their quilts or blankets.

At the other end of the main street, downwind on purpose, stood the livery stable. The blacksmith shop was next to the livery stable, since that was where most of its business was housed.

All the commercial houses lined one side of the street—general store, drug store, clothing store for men and women and children of all ages, a barber shop with a striped pole in front, and a boardinghouse hotel with the saloon next door. They were informal, two-story affairs, with living quarters upstairs and business on the ground floor. The other side of the street contained the public buildings—post office and land claims office, and then, side by side, the bank, courthouse and jail, carrying a not-so-subtle message to bank robbers. In the town's earlier days, a cottonwood tree with sturdy limbs had served as a gallows tree, but with modern times, a permanent wooden gallows stage equipped with a trapdoor and the traditional thirteen steps served as constant reminder for murderers, rapists, and rustlers careless enough to get caught in the act.

Relegated to the back streets was the auto shop with its newfangled Model T Fords, most with rumble seats, and the more commodious Model A Fords, all enclosed by thick board walls to muffle the sputtering and popping noises that made life hell for nervous saddle horses, carriage and buggy trotters, and even the slow-blooded Percherons that hauled the ponderous freight wagons.

There was no mistaking Black Rock Tom's presence that parade day, or any parade day, for that matter. It began with the horses. He favored pintos, which cowboys didn't much care for but Indians did because of their vivid splashes of red and white colors. The real proof of Tom's presence was that every one of his horses had the tips of its ears cropped off. That was an earmark not easily forgotten. It was a sight cowboys would ride for miles to see so that they could swear the story was true without having to risk a lie.

Black Rock Tom's other distinguishing trademarks were his hat, his tomahawk, and his war paint. He wore a round derby hat with slits in the sides, out of which protruded two magnificent eagle feathers earned through bravery. The adornments dangling from the tomahawk he carried had also been earned through bravery. They were made of skin and hair. White men in the valley said they were white scalps, but Ira knew otherwise. He had been living with Cricket at the Paiute campground the night Black Rock Tom came home with them.

The young Paiute braves had been muttering among themselves for some time, complaining that their war chief, Black Rock Tom, had been avoiding the tribe's traditional enemy—the Bannocks—out of fear. The complaints surfaced one night when the braves were gathered around the fire. Without a word, Black Rock Tom had gotten to his feet, tested the edge of his long knife with his thumb, and melted into the darkness. He returned to the fire circle three nights later, materializing almost invisibly out of the darkness. His body was blackened with soot from head to toe, and he was carrying a tomahawk with three bloody Bannock scalps hanging from its shaft. The muttered revolt died that night, and Black Rock Tom's tomahawk became a celebrated totem.

The war paint that distinguished Black Rock Tom from his braves was a gray clay with which he would cover his entire face before the parade. His eyelids were painted black, so that he resembled a death's head. It was a sight that made women cover their eyes and children's mouths drop open.

Only once had Ira seen Indian faces as unforgettable. The three great chiefs of the Paiutes once came to Black Rock Tom's camp to parley. Ira never forgot them—Old Winnemucca whose stone face exuded absolute authority; his brother, Captain Jim, with mad menace in his slit eyes; and Natchez, the peacemaking brother with softness showing in his features. The Paiute warriors who accompanied them had long-boned faces and high cheekbones and lank hair.

Neither Tom nor the braves and women who followed them were painted yet. That would happen when they reached their camping place on the hill overlooking town. None of them was as imaginative as Black Rock Tom when it came to paint. The braves, red skin glistening in the hot sun, were wearing only breechclouts. Their great exploits were depicted in drawings on their bare backs. Eagle, owl, bluejay, and white magpie tail feathers adorned their headdresses. Buckskin hunting shirts decorated with bright designs and fringes covered the upper bodies of some, and pants without seats or crotches covered their hips and legs. Too lazy to drop their pants to take a crap, the white man said of that.

One brave with imagination had been scalped by the Bannocks. Instead of exposing his shame, he had dressed his scalp by fashioning a tight-fitting buckskin cap with a widow's peak and an elaborate pattern of red and blue beads.

The braves were followed by mounted women wearing divided buckskin skirts, something that white female riders would not get around to for a dozen years, being obliged by style to ride uncomfortable sidesaddles. Packhorse loads were light because Indians didn't accumulate things. The biggest dogs wore miniature harnesses across their chests and little packs on their backs.

Last came Ira's friend, Cricket, his black hair stuck up in spikes as it always was and his sharp-boned face as severe

6

as a tomahawk. His eyebrows met above his nose in a straight black line. Beneath them shone black coals of eyes with deep fires burning in their depths. He looked thin, but Ira could attest to his wiriness from their wrestling matches together. Ira was Cricket's absolute opposite with light blond hair, and fair and freckled skin. He was getting tall, giving promise to be as big a man as his father.

White man and Indian met at the exact point of convergence Ira had predicted to himself. He feared that his father was going to force his way through the Indian file, but at the last moment John D. Hamilton by God reined in his big roan and stopped. His level brown eyes met the scowling black eyes of the Indian chief with undisguised challenge.

John D. demonstrated that he didn't care by reaching into his shirt pocket for his sack of Bull Durham and his OCB cigarette papers and nonchalantly rolled a cigarette with one hand, something few men could do on horseback. He was pretty certain that Black Rock Tom couldn't match his feat. John D. Hamilton rubbed it in by lighting the twist of cigarette with the same hand, striking a wooden match with one swipe of the lucifer across his rough Levi's pants. The crisis passed absolutely when Ira's father turned his head away in a gesture that said a confrontation wasn't worth the bother.

When the Paiutes were climbing the hill on the other side, Ira said to his father, "Got to talk to Cricket before the rodeo. I'll catch up with you."

Instead of riding on, John D. Hamilton chose to wait. He heard Ira's whistle and saw Cricket coming back to meet him. The boys had a murmured conversation, and then Cricket turned his Appaloochie, as the cowboys called the breed with the spotted rump, around. Cricket rode bareback in the old Indian way, but the rest of him looked like a white man. He was wearing Ira's outgrown checkered shirt and Levi's worn down to threads. He hadn't given up his moccasins, though. They were newly made, with sturdy soles of badger skin and thongs and the fur turned inside. "He can't make up his mind whether he's going to be white man or Injun," John D. Hamilton thought aloud, and added in a mutter Ira could not hear, "No more than my own son."

At the touch of his heels, Cricket's little Appie, gray with black spotted rear, broke into a lope so light his hooves seemed barely to be touching ground. Ira followed closely behind him as they rode to the head of the column.

Black Rock Tom pulled in his big pinto, and the three talked. The chief's voice was deep and gruff and carried all the way back to John D. Hamilton.

From the edge in his father's voice, Ira decided to play for time, before telling him what his business with Black Rock Tom was really about.

"He likes my horse," said Ira, which was the truth.

"He would," said John D. "Only an Injun would."

Rankled, Ira said bluntly, "I'll need Cricket's help this afternoon."

"There's others that can halter a bronc," said John D. with the familiar edge to his voice. "Injuns ain't the only ones."

"None as fast on their feet as Cricket," said Ira.

"An Injun's still just an Injun," said John D. stubbornly. He reached down to slap the thick leather of his black saddle. "He's not to ride my Visalia," he added proprietarily.

"He won't," said Ira. "I'm the only one who will put legs to that. I'm the bronc rider," he said defensively. "Cricket will do the haltering and the blinding."

Ira knew how much of a sacrifice his father was making.

Borrowing another man's saddle was pushing a relationship to the extreme, even between father and son. Most rodeo saddles were beat-up and patched-up, but John D.'s Visalia was as good as new. John D. had insisted that Ira use it for this one rodeo. Ira knew his father was doing this to protect him from getting hurt, and he was touched. A man would rather loan his best horse than his saddle. *I would bet he would even loan his wife,* Ira almost said aloud, then clamped his mouth and mind shut against an obscene thought like that and went back to straight thinking. In cowboy country like this, a man's saddle was tantamount to owning a crown, and a Visalia-made saddle was like having a jewel in that crown.

A number of things added up to a genuine Visalia—prime leather stretched on the famous Walker oaken saddletree, skirts and fender leather cured for seven years, an intricately wrapped horn that would last a lifetime, bucking rolls swelling out at the perfect angle to wedge a bronc rider's legs in place, a five-inch-high cantle to support the rider's backbone at the rear of the seat, and a cinch and ring placed dead center on a horse's belly, giving the saddle its center-fire name. No wonder a bronc rider would just about sell his soul to have a Visalia center-fire under him at rodeo time. "Once you're locked in that seat," his father had said when he told Ira he could use the Visalia for the Fourth of July rodeo in Sierraville, "it would take a stick of dynamite to blow you out."

Ira hoped his father was right. If John D. Hamilton knew what bronco Ira had defiantly chosen to ride, he might not be so sure.

John D., who would be doing the roping for Ira, was riding a buckskin Morgan horse fifteen hands high and weighing a thousand pounds, with powerful shoulders and strong front legs that could resist the jolt that came when the bronco he lassoed hit the end of the rope. Unlike the Visalia, the saddle he would be using had no bucking rolls on it at all. A roper needed no obstructions against his legs when he climbed on and off his saddle, especially during branding time when he was climbing on and slipping off the saddle fifty times a day, lassoing a calf, dallying the rope around his horn before the calf hit the rope's end, riding the rope down between his hands, upending the calf and tying its four legs together with one of the *piggin* strings looped through his belt. That was real cowboying, to be able to stand up under a beating like that.

Compared to the breeding that had gone into his father's prize Morgan, Ira's horse was no horse at all. He was a non-descript mustang with God-knows-what mix of blood in him. His coloring was nondescript, too, better suited to a calico cat than a horse. That was how one ranch hand had described him the first time he saw him. Hearing it, Ira promptly named his horse Calico. It fit his coloring—gray and black with splashes of red and white.

Calico was unlike John D.'s Morgan in many other ways. He was rawboned, with none of the Morgan's full sleek muscles, and he slouched along with no dignity in his bearing. His presence actually embarrassed John D. Hamilton by God, who felt Ira was letting him down when he had a dozen blooded horses for Ira to choose from.

This was part of the reason Ira had made Calico his horse, to spite his father's show-off railing and his penchant for high breeds. But Ira knew Calico's attributes, and his father didn't. Calico, because he had come from mustang stock, had feet like iron. He never needed to be shod. He could climb or descend the rockiest trail nature could come up with. He could go forever without water, longer than a mule, almost. He could thrive on little feed, and he wasn't choosy about what he ate. He was absolutely fearless, no backing away from a fight ever. In fact, that was one of the reasons Ira had decided to risk life and limb roping him down. When he finally did, the mustang stallion did not run for freedom. He came right at Ira with snorting nostrils and bared teeth. It took every wile Ira knew to hold him at bay, and a few he invented out of desperation.

An old mustanger had told Ira that a mustang once broke would never buck, while a pasture horse was full of surprises and would leave you staring at the sky from your back when you thought you had gone riding to look at the scenery. A mustang might be no roper, no racer, no bulldogger's horse, but he had plenty of just plain grit and a serious attitude toward life.

Secretly in his heart, John D. Hamilton looked down on rodeo cowboys, considering them more performers than cowboys. *Them bronc riders who go from one rodeo to another wouldn't last a week doing real cowboying with me out on the range.* They were "rodeoers," not cowboys, John D. Hamilton by God used to pronounce before he realized more and more of the young cowboys in Heavenly Valley were taking up rodeo riding. Including his own son.

John D. had brought his heavy shotgun chaps, genuine Texas-made, but he would not put them on until rodeo roping time, when his lariat might slip off the dally horn and tear up his legs unless they were protected. Now, his chaps hung loose, draped over the saddle between the horn and the gullet. Being a practical man, he could see no sense in carrying all that leather around on his legs until he needed it.

Like the Visalia saddle, the shotguns were a master's work. Their heavy leather was like armor, meant to last a working cowboy his lifetime. Their wide, double-thick waistband was gracefully engraved, and fringes of leather thongs ran down the sides of the legs. The fringes flapped prettily when a rider was at a trot, but John D. didn't care for that nearly as much as the fact that they provided a supply of leather thongs he could cut off with his knife when there was mending to be done on a worn bridle or latigo strap that bound the horse's belly cinch tight.

Like most of the cattlemen his age, John D. wore high boots with a mule-ear tab to pull them on and a pyramid-crowned hat. His heavy gray hair stuck out from under the brim. A worn cloth vest with plenty of pockets to carry odds and ends also had plenty of room for his arms and shoulders to maneuver in. Around his waist hung a .45 revolver, Smith and Wesson make instead of the Colt's make that was sweeping the West. The pistol was stuffed into a worn-to-death cartridge belt. The butt of the .45 was protected with a buttoned flap to keep trail dust out of the gun's workings. It also told people that he didn't care about being fast on the draw like a gunslick with a revolver in an open holster thonged down on his hip. John D. might draw a second slower, but he made up for that by shooting straight, like people said Wyatt Earp did, letting four bullets fan his cheeks before he fired his first shot, dead center. "If it comes to a shoot-out," John D. said, "I'll see his boots touching air before mine." His yellow slicker, which went wherever he went in all kinds of weather, was tied down with leather straps behind the cantle of his saddle.

In purposeful contrast to his father, Ira's hat was floppy felt that flipped up in front when he was riding into the wind. A sweat ring was climbing higher and higher on the crown. His chaps were batwings, with flaps of leather extending out from thin-cut leggings, which were a darned sight more comfortable than his father's shotguns. That was the new style for the young cowboys in Heavenly Valley, in open defiance to the tight-fitting, heavy-as-chain-mail shotguns his father and grandfather before him had worn. So were Ira's striped shirt and black silk bandana, flashy maybe but distinctive to the young Modoc County cowboys.

They had reached the crest that overlooked Heavenly Valley. John D. Hamilton let out a gasp of exultation as he unfailingly did when he first saw the valley after a time away. For him, it was like discovering the green Promised Land after years of isolation in a gray sagebrush desert. A brutal mountain range served as barrier against the rest of California.

In the green land, great spreading cottonwoods loomed over white frame ranch houses, red barns and sheds, and a maze of pole corrals. Slender poplars stood like tall sentinels in long rows against the direction from which the storms came, breaking the force of winter winds and clouds of drifting snow that would otherwise have clogged the network of lanes and roads connecting the ranches to the wide wagon road along which the tiny towns of Heavenly Valley lay. And most important of all, they looked down on a hundred square miles of emerald-green pasture and alfalfa and wheat fields that would turn golden in autumn, orchards and gardens—veined throughout with fast-moving white water, more water than one could expect to find anywhere in California and neighboring Nevada. The grazing herds of Hereford cattle were fat and sleek, saddle horses and workhorses were glossy with good health, and black and white Holsteins were living insurance of prolific yields of milk, butter, and cheese.

"This is the land our grandfathers found, and our fathers

and us in our turn cleared and plowed and planted," John D. Hamilton intoned as if he were reading holy scripture. "This will be our legacy to you and yours to your children, Ira Hamilton. Guard it with guns from those who would take it away from you. It took hard men to build it, and it will take hard men to hold it. This is our ground, white man's ground," he said in a different voice, but Ira knew what he meant.

You're wrong, Pa, Ira thought to himself. *This was Indian ground first, a thousand years before your grandpa, your pa, and you came along, I will bet.*

It would be a long time before the white man would learn that, and a longer time before he would admit it. But Ira knew. He had learned that lesson through his eyes and his hearing and even the soles of moccasin-covered feet in the one month that he had lived and hunted with Cricket. That adventure had been in the secret sanctuary that by merest chance—or was it something more—having to do with Indian gods? The white man had not discovered it yet, and only the Paiutes knew it existed.

Before that, Black Rock Tom had finally given permission to Cricket to show Ira the secret valley. Until then, Ira Hamilton had believed that the Paiutes of Black Rock Tom were just nomadic Indians, living in the mountains for, say, six months and then picking up when the seasons changed or when the game was gone or the campground all used up with human habitation and moving on to another campsite fifty miles away—usually on the fringes of the great gray deserts that surrounded the green oasis of Heavenly Valley.

Ira Hamilton learned then that the sanctuary Cricket had taken him to was holy ground protected by gods with a little help from nature by way of an almost inaccessible mountain barrier. The paths to it were narrow and twisting and treacherous, discouraging even the first mountain men searching for beaver streams and the settlers searching for a place to raise crops and livestock.

Later, Ira would learn that there was another sanctuary of holy ground a hundred miles away. Surrounded and protected by vast sweeps of desert on which just about the only edible grass was in pockets, like Black Rock Springs that contained a pond thirty yards in diameter. The water in the pond was tepid compared to the boiling springs nearby that would and had, in pioneer wagon days, scalded the flesh off oxen and horses and humans ignorant enough to slide into them.

Humans could bathe and swim in Black Rock Springs without danger of losing their hides. The water that bubbled up from the bottom and spilled over the banks to form rivulets was even drinkable after a cooling distance. Salt grass grew thick and short around the pond, providing soft, springy sleeping ground. The pocket and surrounding desert took their names from a cone of opalized black rock that reared above them. The cone provided more obsidian for arrow and spear points than the Paiutes could use in a dozen lifetimes. It also provided a lookout from which a sentry could see for a hundred miles in every direction.

Black Rock Tom led his band to the springs once every year, mostly in winter when the pocket of steaming water and salt grass against the rock formation could hold its warmth while blizzards raged outside. But survival was not the reason he went. Like the chiefs who had led their bands there before him, Black Rock Tom believed that the first people rose from the bubbling depths millennia ago. So it was holy ground, and the return to it was pilgrimage.

"We have seen our forefathers' bones when the desert god spit them up. Their bones and the bones of animals that walked the earth long ago—but no more."

The proper rites for pilgrimages were performed here. Boys who had reached the beginning of manhood beat the drums in primitive rhythms. Braves painted themselves with shapes of animals that existed no longer, and danced for hours in an unending, mesmerizing circle, women wailed in eerie choruses, and the shamans, imaginations gone wild from chewing peyote cactus buttons, described their hallucinations in keening tones.

This year, Cricket had whispered to Ira, the Paiute band would make the pilgrimage in midsummer instead of winter because of a premonition Black Rock Tom had had. They would leave as soon as the white man's parade and rodeo were done. After the band returned, Cricket and Ira would make their way to the secret valley that was the Paiute sanctuary for all the game a hunter could ask for—deer, antelope, jackrabbits, and cottontail, grouse, quail, sagehen, ducks, geese in migration time, and trout in deep pools. The ground was of course in Cricket's soul memory, and Ira would learn it. It was here that Ira would be taught Indian hunting ways, and the secret of trapping. Cricket would teach him that.

The Paiutes took only what they could eat and smoke and dry on sun racks. If the white man ever discovered the sanctuary, they would kill more than they could ever eat and leave the rest to rot. Everyone, white or Indian, knew how the white men had slaughtered a million buffalo that had provided food and clothing and lodge coverings for a hundred tribes.

When Ira closed his eyes and emptied his mind, he could remember the brush of willows against his bare arms, hear

16

the soft swish of long grass when they crept into the meadow and feel its softness on his bare stomach and legs as he slid like a snake after the slithering form of Cricket. Their quarry was a small bunch of antelope in the meadow. The young hunters held a bow in their left hand, an arrow already nocked to their bowstring, and a bobcat-skin quiver filled snug with arrows slung over their shoulders.

In a month's time, Ira had learned to live Indian. First, he had shed his clothes and stripped to a loincloth and moccasins made out of tough badger skin with the fur inside, adding a rabbitskin jerkin and buckskin leggings only if it got cold at night, and he had learned again to sleep in a buckskin robe. They lighted a small Indian fire at night and dropped small stones into the coals. The stones would then be slipped into watertight bowls woven out of reeds. The bowls held a mixture of seeds, pine nuts, and sun-dried slivers of meat pounded by the women into a gruel. Creek water was poured into the drinking cups, the mixture stirred, and when the stones had heated the gruel, Cricket and Ira first drank the warming broth. Then for strength they scooped up the residue with their fingers. That old staple could sustain them for days if need be, but they were hunters now and needed meat of antelope, deer, and rabbits—all that they had shot and caught, roasted on a spit over the coals. Livers and hearts they ate raw, chewing with the blood spilling over their lips. Hearts squeezed for blood went to daub their arms and legs.

Ira had learned how to make pitfall and deadfall traps for small game. For bigger game, he learned how to fashion the ultimate weapon—bow and arrow. The best wood for a hunting bow was a yew or alder limb, five feet long and filled with strong supple life. The limb was scraped smooth with a sanding stone out of Cricket's pouch of miniature tools, and reinforced at its pressure points with thin strips of sinew from a deer's leg. The sinew was wrapped when it was green, so that it constricted as it dried until it was immovable. Feathers were tipped into hair-thin grooves at the rear of the arrow shaft. The slits were filled with droplets of a unique liquid cement. The fluid was scraped off the inside of a rattlesnake's skin. It dried so quickly that a hundred arrow shafts had to be feathered at the same time. Once the feathers were attached, there was no manipulating them. It was as if they had grown out of the shaft. That formula had supposedly been found by the Choctaw Indians to the southeast and spread rapidly through the western Indian tribes whose hunting ground possessed a multitude of rattlesnakes.

The making of arrowheads was an art in itself. Flakes of the glasslike stone were broken off a chunk of black obsidian rock, shaped to proper size by the tribe's arrowmakers, serrating the edges of the projectile-to-be. Obsidian was the favored stone for arrow points for other reasons than its workability. If the arrow point hit a bone of an enemy, white or red, it would splinter like glass, tearing at flesh and mortifying it finally. Unlike the white man's bullet, which could be cut out, the arrow fragments were plain hell to remove.

For life-or-death battles, all a brave had to do was jab an arrow point into a deer's liver that had been saturated by a dozen strikes of a rattlesnake.

The final advantage of the bow and arrow was its silent flight. A brave could kill a deer or an enemy without alerting others of his find. A rifle bullet announced the presence of an armed white man with one thundering crash of noise.

At the end of a month, Ira was nearly as Paiute as Cricket. He could crouch for an hour without a muscle stirring in the concealment of long grass, then rise suddenly to an upright stance and sink an arrow clear to its feathers in a fully grown buck.

They awoke in the darkness and moved out into the "yellow light" of dawn, as the Paiutes called it, when deer and skipping antelope and big cottontail rabbits began to stir. At noonday, when the sun discouraged movement in the wild, Ira learned to rest like an Indian, he and Cricket making the air about them blue, indulging in their mutual vice. They mixed white man's Bull Durham with Indian tobacco in corn-shuck paper and smoked cigarettes one after the other until they were dizzy and sated.

At the end of day, when the cool time began, they ventured out again, following the leaf-shaded game trails of a century and more. When the trails reached out onto the plain, Cricket was at his hunting best, actually bounding so fast he could catch a jackrabbit with his hands.

When the month was done, Ira and Cricket left the secret valley and made their way through the labyrinth of passages that led to the outside. Ira could not see it in himself, but John D. Hamilton did. Ira had begun to think and feel and move like an Indian. Something had happened to his soul, and it showed in his eyes.

Ira Hamilton's body had fused with the soul of the Indian. He was as much an Indian as a white man.

The giant firecracker that signaled the start of the Fourth of July celebration had been encased in a large Hills Brothers coffee can to double the sound of its explosion. It did more than that. The shattering roar exceeded everyone's expectations when it was set off in the middle of the wide dirt street that fronted the reviewing stand. The Hills Brothers coffee can catapulted end over end straight up in the air. Fortunately, it did not fly sideways into the dignitaries that filled the reviewing stand. Luckily, too, there were no horses within immediate earshot of the explosion. They had been removed to the empty lot behind the livery stable. Otherwise, there would have been an uncalled-for rodeo and stampede in the middle of the street.

From out of the melee of horses, floats, painted Indians,

and costumed people gathered in the lot, the Grand Marshal emerged first.

He was riding a big black horse whose nerves were obviously frayed by the commotion surrounding him. His ebony skin was glistening with sweat, his mouth was white with froth, his head was tossing against the silver-studded martingale that kept his chin down, protecting the Grand Marshal's teeth from getting knocked out, and his gait was something between single footing and sideways dancing.

Ira regarded the horse's antics with disapproval. He glanced up at his father standing beside him among the spectators lining the street. John D. Hamilton's judging eyes reinforced Ira's sentiments.

When the Grand Marshal passed the red-white-and-blue bunting-covered reviewing stand with its myriad American flags, he stood up in his tapaderoed stirrups and doffed his big white hat. From the stand, the mayor reciprocated in kind by tipping his black silk top hat. He was dressed in a black broadcloth suit that Ira figured must have been pure torture in the broiling July sun. His lady beside him was dressed more sensibly in a gauzy muslin dress and a white bonnet. Nevertheless, a trickle of perspiration had worked its way down her powdered cheek. Occasionally, she dabbed at it with a dainty white silk handkerchief.

Following the Grand Marshal's lead, the parade entries fell into line—Spanish-American War veterans in faded blue uniforms following with faltering steps the Stars and Stripes and the Bear Flag of California; the Sierraville band in red coats and white crossbelts blaring Sousa marches with trumpets and cornets and a booming bass drum drowning out a tenor singing *America* from the stand; a horse-drawn flatbed float with corn shucks and bales of hay and gingham-clad girls with sunny smiles boasting Heavenly Valley's flourishing farm crops; a Rotary float bearing a miniature log cabin and a buckskin-clad frontiersman with a moth-eaten coonskin cap and a long flintlock musket standing with one foot on the neck of a prone Indian who was really a white man painted red; a cavalcade of that new contraption called an automobile, Model T and Model A Fords with shining coats of paint, chrome trim and massive headlights, and squeeze-bulb horns going ooo-gah, scaring any horse that happened to be nearby, tiny American flags fluttering from their hood ornaments, driven by downtown gigolos in straw hats, linen dusters, and goggles, and one of the passengers jumping out at every stop to dust off the chrome trim and new paint job; then Black Rock Tom with his death's-head coating of gray warpaint, followed by half-naked braves on red-and-white-splashed pinto mustangs and spotted Appaloosa horses; and finally, the free entries, the cowboys of Heavenly Valley and wherever, wearing batwing chaps and shotgun chaps and hair chaps, and to a man, white shirts with black silk scarves and red arm garters.

John D. Hamilton's eyes were focused on the outline of a tin cup branded into the flank of a parade horse. "That's a rustled hoss. I know that brand. I seen it in Oregon."

Ira's gaze followed his father's to the brand and then over the man riding the horse. He was lean as whipcord, with a long skeletal face marred by nicks from a straight razor, as if he had washed and shaved especially for the parade. A black moustache hung down on either side of a narrow-lipped mouth. A black neckerchief was wrapped around his throat. The rest of him was black, too, from hat to leather vest to cartridge belt and holster, and winged chaps studded like a poker hand—spade, heart, club, and diamond.

Down to his saddle and bridle, he was a study in black.

As a final touch, the unknown cowboy carried a short rawhide whip attached to his left wrist by a leather thong, ostensibly to train horses but, as occasion had proven, handy to blind an adversary with a backhand flip of his wrist for those few seconds necessary to draw his pistol first.

John D. Hamilton spit contemptuously into the dirt street. "Anyone who goes to all that trouble to look dangerous don't scare me one bit. Now, if he was a decent-dressed man doing his damnedest not to look mean, but with that look in his eyes, I would watch out for him. This man is a sidewinder, the kind of rattler you can't tell what direction he will come at you."

John D. Hamilton's spitting into the street had not gone unnoticed by the rider in black. He turned his head and stared threateningly at the rancher. His slitted eyes took in John D.'s powerful build, the .45 revolver stuffed into a well-worn holster, and finally the regard with which John D. Hamilton held him. The rustler's expression lost its resolution.

There was a sudden commotion of clapping hands, whistles, and hoots from three men standing together on the other side of the street. In contrast to the townsfolk and ranchers who had spruced up for the holiday, they were unshaven and grimy, as if they had had a token wash at some pump on the outskirts of town. Dust was caked like a mud pack on the creases of their hats and chaps. *Trail dust,* thought Ira. *They've been on the road and in a hurry.* While the three went to the festivities in Sierraville, they had for sure hidden their stolen goods—horses—in some canyon. A rope fence with fluttering rags was enough to keep them there, John D. Hamilton knew.

"Hey, Hawkeye!" one of them shouted. "You're beautiful."

The rider in black welcomed the diversion from John D.'s wordless challenge. Sweeping off his black hat, he made an exaggerated bow to his companions.

"That's a rustler, and his friends are rustlers," John D. Hamilton said in a carrying voice. "They look like critters who will throw a wide loop and catch anything that's under it. You can smell 'em a mile off. A short drop from a tall tree is the way they'll end up."

John D. Hamilton knew the habits of rustlers. They stole horses in one state and sold them in another, all the way from the Canadian border down through Washington, Oregon, Idaho, California, Nevada, Arizona, New Mexico, and into Mexico. Along the way, they did business with ranchers whose consciences didn't bother them when it came to building their horse herds. If put to the test, John D. Hamilton would have to own up he had made a few good buys from them. The return trip from Mexico was hazardous. The Mexican grandees and their vaqueros were not reluctant when it came to shooting rustlers, or worse, enclosing them in green rawhide that would squeeze their blood and eyes out when it dried in the hot sun.

Hawkeye's friends might have made something out of John D. Hamilton's words. But what happened next was so unexpected that it halted movement all along the parade route.

The Grand Marshal had doubled back to the lot where the parade entrants had congregated. Nobody saw him go into the dark cavern of the livery stable, dismount and open a gate to an immaculately clean stall, and emerge leading a horse whose like few, if anybody, in Heavenly Valley had seen before.

He was pearl gray in color with a mane so fine that it seemed to be made of silver threads. His rump was speckled with charcoal spots. Short-coupled, he tossed his arched neck only infrequently. But what was most singular about him was his stride. His legs moved as if he were trotting through water. He was an Arabian, and he might as well have been moving through a sea of Sahara sand.

Sensing something, John D. Hamilton looked down at his son. To his astonishment, he saw that Ira's cheeks were wet with tears. Involuntarily, John D.'s big hand reached out to clasp his son's shoulder. The boy's frame was shivering. John D.'s nature would not permit him to go further in recognizing the depth of his son's emotions.

The Grand Marshal reined to a halt in front of the reviewing stand. The mayor handed him the loudspeaker.

"This here horse is an Ay-rab. He will go to the winner of today's bronc-riding competition," the Grand Marshal's voice boomed out.

A moccasined foot edged over to touch Ira's boot. Ira turned his head to see that Cricket had slipped through the spectators to join him. Cricket's eyes met Ira's. He whispered in Paiute, "We will win him."

Ira's mouth was trembling so that he could not speak. But his chin was firm as he nodded assent.

At the end of the parade route, Hawkeye was stepping down out of the saddle. At the growing crowd noise, he turned to hear the Grand Marshal's announcement and see the Arab toss his silver mane.

"Before this day is done," he said hoarsely. "One way or t'other, that Ayrab will be mine."

3

John D. Hamilton by God, standing stiff as a statue on the platform that looked down on the bronc and bull riders' pit, could make out no recognizable features, only a cluster of crowns and wide brims of cowboy hats.

The ground around them was a tangle of leather—frayed and discarded latigo straps; belly cinches; heavy black leather halters with brass rings at the junctures; reins old and new, strengthened by thongs cut off the fringes of shotgun chaps like the ones John D. Hamilton wore, and rebraided riatas. Knives and hole punchers and pliers gripped by calloused hands flashed in the afternoon sun.

The muffled snatches of conversation that rose from the bronc and bull riders' pit had to do with riders and animals, naturally:

"I've seen cowboys in Wyoming make a bucking roll out

of a thick round stick wrapped with blanket strips and thonged down. Saved a rodeoer's thighs from all that banging from a bucking hoss. They called it a Cheyenne roll."

"I've seen wild steers in Nevada that could outrun a roping horse."

"'Once at a rodeo in old Mexico,' like the song goes, I seen ropers who would rope past a steer, grab its tail and dally it around their horns. But they had to give it up. Broke too many steers' necks."

"For my money, the Spanish boys, Mexicans, and Niggers was the best rodeoers. Afraid of nothing."

John D. Hamilton suddenly remembered the best bronc rider of them all. Because he was a black man, the rules didn't let him ride for prizes. But he made more money by this trick: He would get on a mean bronc and have someone slip a $20 gold piece between the sole of his boot and the bottom of the stirrup. If he rode out a minute without letting that gold piece fall out, he could keep it. By the end of a rodeo, he would make himself a nice piece of change.

John D. was reminiscing when the cowboy talk below took on a subdued tone. He could barely hear a muttered, "Look at that son of a bitch with the fancy chaps." He followed their gaze. In the corner of the bronc riders' pit, the cowboy he had called a rustler was sitting cross-legged on the ground. He was hunched over as if concealing what he was up to. But from his vantage point, John D. Hamilton could see. The rustler deserved to be called a son of a bitch. He was filing his spurs to a point that would send his bronc sky high. No matter that the bronc he was riding would be dripping blood from raking spurs. The judges would see what was happening. If there was to be any penalty to be exacted, they were the ones to exact it.

*　*　*

With the end of the parade, Sierraville had exploded with activity. On a perfectly flat piece of ground on one side of Main Street, a baseball diamond had been marked out with lime on dirt. The bases were canvas sacks filled with gravel, and home plate was staked down. There was a pitcher's mound splattered with tobacco juice. Following tradition, the baseball players, particularly the pitcher, had a quid of tobacco in their mouths. Between pitches, the pitcher chawed and spat. The pitcher was dressed in knickers and striped shirt, a billed cap and a worn glove. He walked to the plate with a sauntering gait. Since the game was slow paced, spectators sat on buckboards and hay wagons. Footraces were held on the other side of Main Street, involving the fleet-footed of all ages from ten to twenty. After that age, the runners diminished in speed and endurance.

Spectators at each event varied according to their profession and relationships. Merchants and shop clerks and their wives dominated at the baseball game, the men in soft, low-heeled lace-and-button shoes, bowties, and straw hats, the women demure with ankles crossed beneath their long gingham and calico dresses, sitting on rumble seats of roadsters and improvised benches on the flatbeds of hay trucks.

Fathers and uncles, willingly or unwillingly, there to watch their sons and nephews, dominated the spectators lining the footrace tracks. Here, too, straw hats and soft shoes were proper attire.

But as always, it was the rodeo that drew by far the most spectators. There were no bleachers, but every inch of space was taken. Men from town and country sat on the top rails of the sturdy fence that surrounded the immense arena that would hold the bronc and bull riding and bulldogging. Almost to a man, the spectators were ranchers, working cowboys, rodeoers, and ranch hands. Wide-brimmed hats with sombrero brims, Stetsons all, and crowned hats with short brims, the kind John D. Hamilton's generation clung to. Denim Levi's reinforced at the stress points by copper rivets seemed almost obligatory. Everybody who worked with livestock wore them. The custom of the day was to fold them up at the bottom. Cowboy boots with high heels finished off what amounted to rodeo costume. But the high heels had a practical use besides keeping a boot from sliding through a stirrup. The cowboys who came to watch hooked their high heels on a lower rung of the fence they were sitting on. If a bronc or a bull took it in mind to scrape a rider off against the fence, which was not uncommon, they had no qualms in scraping off a spectator or two whose dangling boots were fair game. With high heels, the cowboys could propel themselves over backwards out of harm's way.

The rodeo began with no prelude but the crash of hind feet splintering the side boards of the bronc chute. An unpretty mustang stallion with a Roman nose and bunched masses of muscle exploded snorting into the arena, bent only on regaining his freedom.

Seconds later, John D. Hamilton's powerful Morgan roping horse leaped out of the adjoining chute. In contrast to the mustang stallion, the Morgan's gait was trained, his breeding showed, and he had a purpose in mind. John D. Hamilton had delayed his pursuit only long enough to size up the bronc's speed and twisting direction.

In that few seconds delay, John D. Hamilton had already started shaking out his rawhide riata. Now, he shook out the rest of his loop and began his twirl.

Knowing what was to come, the bronc had already started bucking, accomplishing nothing but slowing down his straightaway speed. The loop had hardly settled around his neck when John D. Hamilton dallied his lariat around his saddle horn and pulled up on the reins. The Morgan's stanchion legs straightened and stiffened, and his great hooves plowed like shovels into the dirt.

The bronc hit the end of John D. Hamilton's lariat with such force that he almost turned a somersault. When he had gotten his feet under him again, he began to prove why no rider had ever been able to cope with the coiled gyrations of his neck and body. Finally, he realized that he could not shake off the rawhide bond that encircled his neck. On his part, John D. Hamilton did not let up on the coil, but followed the old roper's classic dictum that a little choking won't hurt the bronc but help the rider. "He needs weakening" was the rationale.

What followed was a spectacle the rodeo crowd had never seen before. His four legs churning in reverse, the mustang stallion literally tried to pull the Morgan roping horse forward onto his knees. It was a tugging match between two colossal animals.

The outcome would never be known.

Running on moccasined feet, Cricket darted across the intervening space between the bronc riders' pen and the two horses caught up in a tug of war. Looped over one shoulder was a bridle of heavy black leather, brass rings and a short thick cotton rope. Clutched in his other hand was a burlap sack cut to pull up over the stallion's eyes.

Startled by the apparition of the Indian on foot, the stallion paused for an instant in his pulling against the Morgan roping horse. In that instant, a flurry of things happened. John D. Hamilton backed up his powerful Morgan, tightening the rawhide lariat around the stallion's throat, cutting off his air. Simultaneously, Cricket pulled the fitted burlap hood over the bronc's nose and jerked upwards until it covered his eyes. Blinded, the bronc stopped all movement and stood shock still.

In that instant, Ira burst from the bronc chute. In two leaps, his horse had joined the melee. Cricket fitted the heavy bridle to the bronc's head. Ira skidded to a stop. He leaped off his horse, pulling his father's Visalia saddle off his horse and letting the blanket slip to the ground. He heaved the saddle over the bronc's back and cinched it as best he could. He swung into the saddle and caught the thick cotton rope Cricket tossed to him. It would be the only rein he would have in the bucking to come.

When Ira was settled in the saddle, Cricket pulled the burlap blinding hood from under the bridle. There was a collective gulping of breath from a hundred cowboy spectators perched on the fence. They knew what was to come. John D. Hamilton's face hardened into granite lines of disapproval. He had vented his incredulity in no uncertain terms when it was announced that Ira had demanded to ride the mustang stallion. He was not alone. The cowboy crowd whistled and hooted, and some even laughed when they heard. In ten years of Heavenly Valley rodeos, nobody had managed to stick on Thunder longer than five jumps, and most not even that. There were few riders damn fool enough to match their skills against a horse that was born to buck and raised to buck. From the time Thunder threw his first rider, his owners, who specialized in the business of raising bucking horses, knew they had in the powerful mustang the best of three generations of buckers. Even the Indian elders nodded in agreement that he was like the horses of times before whose main weapon of survival was to throw off the mountain lion who had sprung down from his high rock, gotten a hold on his quarry with four taloned paws, and gouged with razored fangs seeking to sever the spinal cord.

Once rid of the rider on his back, Thunder, like his fore-bearers, doubled back to stomp a fallen cowboy with hard, outsized hooves.

Thunder stood still until his vision had cleared and he realized there was a rider and a saddle on his back. Then he exploded.

Instead of bucking straight up, he gathered his muscles and took two long jumps forward, gaining momentum with each jump until he was airborne. He landed with his front legs stiff, his front hooves digging into the dirt. Only the Visalia saddle's rigid bucking rolls kept Ira from being thrown forward over the bronc's lowered head. Ira knew his thighs would be black and blue for a week after. But the worst was yet to come. Thunder's fore quarters reared forward, his hind quarters leaped forward also, and Ira thought his back was broken from the impact of the cantle against his spine.

Thunder repeated his combination forward thrust and lifting hind quarters five more times. Ira was beyond feeling pain by then, but his blurred vision told him they had crossed the arena before the bronc switched his tactic. Thunder tried to scrape his rider off with a glancing run down the length of the fence. Spectators tumbled like ten-pins backwards off the fence. Again, it was a combination of human instinct, his batwing chaps, and the Visalia saddle's thick fenders that saved Ira from having his left leg crushed by the bronc's glancing swipes down the length of the fence. Grabbing the horn as an anchor, Ira lifted his left leg clear and made the ride with all his weight on the right-side stirrup.

When all else had failed, Thunder pulled the final weapon out of his arsenal. He reared straight up so that his forefeet were pawing the air over his head. Deliberately, he threw himself on his back in one last attempt to crush the insect that clung to him so tenaciously.

It was instinct alone that saved Ira this time. When he knew for certain what Thunder intended to do, he grasped the bucking rolls and shoved himself sideways off the saddle. Instinct also landed him on his feet with the thick cotton halter rope still in his hand.

Thunder was not so lucky. His final tactic missed its purpose of crushing the rider at too great a cost. The jolt of heavy horse being hurled against unyielding ground knocked the air out of his lungs and the last of his strength out of his body. Thunder scrambled weakly to his feet, and as he rose, Ira stepped into the saddle and rose with him. Thunder made one last feeble attempt to buck, but all he could muster were a few crow hops that would not have dislodged a child.

Finally, Thunder gave up. He came to a stop, his torso heaving, his head bowed nearly to the ground, his legs tottering under him, the mucous pouring from his nostrils was laced now with blood.

Ira stepped out of the saddle. At first, his legs would not hold him. He was unable to stand without support. To keep from falling, he wrapped his arms around Thunder's neck. The battle was done. Ira felt no elation. He could not even hear the crescendo of yelping and yipping and cheering from his peers of the cowboy crowd that lined the arena. He rested his forehead against Thunder's neck, and his tears mingled with the dripping sweat of the horse. Ira's body was shaking with an immense sadness. Together, they stood as if they had been sculpted out of the same piece of clay.

And then a strange thing happened. The yelping and the cheering from the spectators quieted. Creased eyes set into leathered range faces stared downward to conceal their emotion. It was a tribute of silence to a young cowboy with only grit and determination as weapons and a magnificent animal whose unconquerable spirit had at last been broken.

Whatever else that was to follow would be unimportant. The rodeo was over.

"I guess we better get acquainted," said Ira in a voice to match the gentle touch of his fingertip as it stroked the lower lid of the Arab's eye.

Afterwards, he let his hand rub the Arab's body from the muzzle down the pearl-gray length of his back to his spotted rump. He was especially careful with the Arab's finely muscled legs, lifting each hoof by a tug on its fetlock to get him used to the way Ira would check his feet.

It was an exercise Ira had learned from a Paiute elder whose way with horses had won him a wide reputation. Not many hot-blooded braves had the patience to keep up the practice for more than a week or so, but those who rubbed their ponies by hand from when they were foals to grown adults would have horses that would never buck and who would respond to every touch of a heel or a single rawhide rein. From the beginning, their war ponies became as much a part of them as their arms or legs.

Ira had managed to get into the stall that held the Arab by approaching with as little noise as possible. When he reached the gate to the stall, he talked softly to his newly won horse. "I'm not going to give you any fancy name. I'm going to call you what you are—Ayrab." When the Arab had gotten used to Ira's voice, the boy held out a bribe—a long carrot. The Arab sniffed the carrot's tip, then took a tentative bite. Grinding the morsel of carrot seemed to give him pleasure, and he finished the whole carrot a bite at a time.

Ira's stroking of the pony must have had a mesmerizing effect. The Arab's eyes actually began to droop, and Ira's with him. Ira was tired, he realized now. The bronc ride had been enough to exhaust even a hardened rodeoer. He was barely able to walk by the time he had led the Arab to the livery stable and put him in a stall with clean-smelling straw for bedding, and hay for eating. But he walked dutifully to the long line of barbecue tables filled with big round bowls of potato and macaroni salads, platters of barbecued beef and lamb in thick slices, pork sausages, still-steaming rolls, and pitchers of punch, coffee, and milk.

Ira was almost too tired to eat, but to make the gauntlet of the barbecue table was obligatory. He accepted the slaps of congratulations from callused hands on his back and shoulders, but even more important was the new regard he saw in the eyes of these range riders, who were hard judges of men. Ira had passed from boy to man in one afternoon. The affectionate hugs and kisses of women who were as old as his mother would have been, had she lived, he accepted with an unexplained longing.

There was only one embrace Ira was really waiting for, but for a secret reason that would have sent John D. Hamilton by God a mile high in the air. Her name was properly Molly; she was slender, with barely budding breasts and a dusting of freckles across her nose and cheeks. Molly was sunny and shy, and she actually blushed when she said memorized lines, "My mother and father said I should reward you with a kiss for winning the bronc riding today." Ira bent his head obligingly, and her lips brushed his cheek so fleetingly he felt nothing.

Ira supposed he would marry Molly one day. She was the daughter of a prosperous rancher and was already learning how to bake bread and make cakes, and to put up preserves. She knew kitchen duties, and she was said to be a wizard with needle and thread and had handmade quilts to prove it.

Molly would have been scandalized if she knew what was passing through Ira's memory like a hot poker burning its way through gauze.

Enveloped by darkness broken only by the moon and stars, they were lying on a rabbitskin quilt. Ira was looking down on a girl with honey-colored skin and raven hair and lynx eyes that smoldered with passion. The dusky smell of her suffused his senses. It was a blend of wildness and young womanhood and lovemaking and Indian.

She was Thoma, Cricket's sister, the daughter of Black Rock Tom. Almost from the beginning, Black Rock Tom and his wife knew what was happening between Ira and Thoma, and approved, not in blatant words but with their eyes and touch. After that, when Black Rock Tom and his wife touched Ira, there was possession in their embraces.

It was inevitable that their love for each other must one

day be consummated. They were powerless to resist. It was as though the gods had willed it.

When Ira and Thoma first stripped and lay down on the soft fur of the rabbitskin blanket, they lay side by side with only their hips touching. All their senses were heightened by a new awareness of each other, of possibilities unknown until this moment. Their breathing quickened almost imperceptibly. A new hunger grew in them, grew and grew, but they would not yield to it until it was time. Then Ira's hand delicately stroked her silken skin, the smooth lines and hollows of her legs, and the unbelievable tenderness of an inner thigh. Slowly they discovered each other anew with their hands and lips, and as their yearning grew, so did their love.

When Thoma could contain herself no longer, her legs intertwined with Ira's, and he lifted his body to cover hers. She raised herself up to meet the full length of him, and her thighs opened to receive him. Slowly and gently, he penetrated her, both of them gasping with the wonder of it, the consuming ecstasy of their love. Their bodies fused in instinctive rhythm and desire. Then her surrender began with the first distant little moan that grew louder until there was one moan of human ecstasy blended with the scream of a wildcat. She arched her neck forward, and Ira felt her teeth biting into the flesh of his shoulder. It was then that Ira surrendered to her passion, planting in her innermost being a seed that would never die.

Afterward, they lay side by side on the rabbitskin blanket, their energy gone and only the smear of blood on his shoulder and around her mouth remained. That and the secret seed that was already joined. They were enveloped by dream stuff that led to deep sleep.

When they awakened, she whispered to Ira that she had

opened her eyes and saw the stars and the moon smiling in approval.

Ira continued to look at Molly as though he were transfixed by her passionless blue eyes. But his attention was far away. No matter if he married Molly or anyone else of her kind, nothing could equal that night on a rabbitskin under stars and moonlight. He decided then and there that he was making no promises to convention.

5

"There is absolutely no mistaking the sound of a nickel-plated cartridge being levered into the metal breech of a rifle. It is the most lethal sound in the world, because it speaks of death. And the quieter the sound, the louder its message."

John D. Hamilton by God had intoned this scripture to Ira on the day he taught his son how to arm and shoot his .30-30 Winchester carbine. He illustrated his sermon by actually going through the motions with his carbine. The gun was like a toy in his big hands. "Now, listen, son," he had ordered Ira. "I will arm this weapon as quietly as I can. But I will bet you can hear the sound of its warning a quarter mile away."

Never one to let opportunity slip by, John D. Hamilton simultaneously taught Ira the right way to shoot a pistol. Not the Smith and Wesson .45, because cartridges were too expensive to waste, but with a .22 pistol of the same make as a Colt's Peacemaker. John D. showed Ira how to stand sideways so as to offer the thinnest target for his adversary, how to pull the hammer back on the upswing and let go his charge when the gun barrel came down—a straight line from shoulder to front sight of the pistol. When Ira tried the heavy .45 revolver, he learned respect for the damage it could do, blowing a big can all to hell. He learned how to lead a moving target by aiming at the most difficult of all targets, a jackrabbit bounding every which way, far more elusive than a man.

John D. Hamilton had been right, and Ira had been right in sensing the rustlers would try to steal the colt. The truth of the sermon reached Ira for the first time as he crouched in a stall in the livery stable and levered the cartridge into the breech of the carbine. The snick was as quiet as he could muster, but it seemed to screech like a banshee in the vaulted darkness of the stable, louder than the hooting of an owl in the rafter. Instantly, all the little sounds he had heard fell quiet, the scuff of a boot sole on the rough planking of the floor, the muted jingle of a spur rowel, even the deep breathing of the rustlers. When the gun was loaded, he thrust the barrel through the aperture between two of the side boards of the stall. Fitting the stock to his shoulder, he pointed the muzzle at the wide square of pale light that showed where the double doors to the stable were. The silhouette of a man outlined there froze into immobility and then vanished with a sideways leap into the darkness.

There was silence for several seconds. "They're waiting," Ira said to himself. "But I'm waiting, too. I'll see them before they see me."

The rustlers must have reached the same conclusion.

There was a whistling intake of breath and the scraping of boots and spurs as the rustlers crept out of the stable. Ira added a silent thanks to his father for the lesson he had taught him.

The presence of the rustlers did not come as much of a surprise to Ira. He had caught glimpses of them twice since the rodeo had ended—badly for Hawkeye. The lean-faced rustler with the stringy moustache and the batwing chaps had drawn a tough bronco, but his raking of the mustang's flanks with honed-down spur points was too much even for judges not squeamish about the sight of blood. They had reprimanded and disqualified him. Hawkeye's tirade made no impression upon them at all.

When the rodeo was over, Ira had led the prize Arab to his stall in the livery stable. The stable was safe ground, full of activity as ranchers groomed parade horses and checked harnesses on family buggies. Ira stalled the Arab and looked longingly at the inviting stack of straw where he planned to sleep.

Prodded by an ingrained sense of duty to tell his father what he had done, and the music from the Grange hall, Ira sighed and went to tell John D. that the Arab was stalled. Ira nodded hello to the cowboys and townsmen gathered around the barrel of whiskey occupying its traditional place outside the hall. Even though the saloon was only a few steps away, local custom on rodeo day dictated that the male gentry of Heavenly Valley buy a pint of whiskey ranging from good corn liquor to rotgut and pour its contents into the outside barrel. Custom also dictated that cowboys and store clerks alike drink from a wooden dipper whose curved handle was hooked on the rim of the barrel when not in use.

Ira would ordinarily have paid no attention to the circle of cowboys swapping stories exaggerated by booze, but one cowboy's raucous laugh got his attention. It was Hawkeye's. Ira passed him by and clumped up the steps to the dance floor. He saw his father dancing with the plump widow with whom he always danced. Rumor had it that John D. Hamilton and the widow would one day marry, but such weighty affairs took a long time in slow-paced Heavenly Valley. Ira took off his hat in politeness and said hello to the widow, then leaned close to his father's ear and told him all was well with the Arab at the livery stable.

But all was not well, and Ira had his suspicion confirmed when he went outside and passed the whiskey barrel again. Hawkeye and his rough-looking friends tried to look away in time, but not soon enough. Ira's disquiet returned strongly enough to make him stop by the saddle racks and pull his father's Winchester out of its scabbard and check its load. Then he returned to the livery stable to wait.

Once Ira had frightened them from the stable, the rustlers did not return. Ira went to sleep on the golden straw with the Winchester beside him, his head resting on his father's yellow slicker. Ira's hand still lay on the carbine when John D. Hamilton nudged him awake at sunrise with the toe of his boot, signaling that it was time to begin the long ride back home to the ranch.

When they had ridden past the last building on the outskirts of Sierraville, they mounted to the wide wagon road. The Arab trailed along behind Ira on his fancy lead rope.

Rock formations flanked the road on the uphill side. This time, it was John D. Hamilton's turn to waken his instincts. Without explanation, he unsheathed his Winchester carbine and handed it to Ira. Ira checked to see if there was a cartridge in the chamber. There was, and he levered the breech closed and propped the gun crosswise on the saddle, ready for action. Simultaneously, John D. checked his heavy revolver, making sure it was filled with its blunt-nosed cartridges.

While his father scanned the concealing rock on the uphill side, Ira did the same on the sagebrush clumps below the wagon road. Just in case, he held the Winchester in both hands.

6

The Hamilton homestead rested in the first of a chain of unexpected meadows with a creek winding through it. At daybreak, deer came down to the creek to dip their velvet muzzles into the clear cold water. The Hamiltons' old shepherd dog had once chased them, but eventually gave up and watched the deer through dozing eyes instead.

On one side of the topmost meadow was a long line of aspen trees bearing thick clusters of leaves that trembled with the slightest breath of wind. Their other distinctive trait was trunks that shone white on moonlit nights. The aspen had been planted by nature and remained nurtured by her.

The north side of the meadow where the ranch house sat had been planted by John D. Hamilton's grandfather when he homesteaded this parcel of the West many years before. John D.'s cattle fed on the adjoining public land, alternating with periodic times of grazing on the ranch's own meadow grass. The rest of the meadows were planted in alfalfa that was cut scrupulously by John D. and his son three times in summer and autumn. The spring growth was given over to grazing because there was little nourishment in it.

On the unprotected side of the big meadow, the sagebrush began, running up the mountain slopes to a brown buttress of rimrock. The bare walls of rock below the rim were pockmarked with holes that served as caves for the small varmints of the desert and a dozen species of songbirds and meat-hunting hawks. The erosion of ages had given the rimrock strange shapes, many of them like perfect cones of white chalk. The cones had an air of softness, but the dominant trait of the rimrock was harsh cruelty.

At the beginning of the chain of meadows there was a little protected hollow ringed to the north by poplars and cottonwoods. The poplars served as a barrier against the winter winds and snowstorms that came from the north, and the cottonwoods covered the Hamilton house with a canopy of leafy shade against the broiling suns of summer.

The house where John D. Hamilton and his son lived was actually a log cabin that had been extended several times through almost three generations of Hamiltons. To the original kitchen and sleeping cabin, separate rooms had been added so that the kitchen had its own place, and the bedrooms were small but separated. Over time, a room that had been intended as a parlor had become a museum of sorts. It was filled with the trappings of westering—oxen yokes worn smooth by the long journey from the jumping-off place in Missouri for pioneers heading west, oaken hames with polished steel knobs, heavy harnesses to pull the covered wagons, a disordered array of saddles, bridles, bits, and spurs, shotguns, fowling pieces, ponderous Sharps buffalo guns, elongated Colt Patterson and Navy Colt revolvers, most still in working order.

One corner of the kitchen contained a pantry with sturdy shelves from ceiling to floor to hold oversized cans of coffee beans, sugar, and salt, and enough spices to tide the household over during the months when winter snows would clog the wagon road to town and markets. When Sarah Hamilton lived, other shelves had been stacked with Mason jars filled with pears and peaches, all of which came from her garden on the kitchen side of the house so as to be handy to get at when putting-up time came. The shelves had depleted sadly after Sarah died.

Off to one side of the house there was a stone walkway that led to a root cellar half buried in the earth. Stone steps led downward to the thick cellar door. The stone floors of the root cellar were littered with potatoes and turnips. Hams and bacon covered with salt and cayenne pepper hung in shrouds from the rafters. Hind quarters of beef also hung ready for the butchering knife when John D. Hamilton and Ira had a yen for steaks, which was often. John D. had also become a fair hand at preparing stews filled with beef chunks, potatoes, and onions.

One side of the root cellar held great blocks of ice cut in winter from the river and covered with sawdust to slow the melting. The ice blocks were flanked by kegs of beer for the Saturday nights when John D. Hamilton and a handful of neighboring ranchers undaunted by distance would gather for tall mugs of beer and taller stories.

Beyond the house and the root cellar stood a hay and feed barn. The loft was stuffed with nourishing green hay from the Hamilton fields, enough to pitch down to wagon beds in those frequent winters when the snow was too deep for cattle and horses to paw down through it to find food. Ever since the disastrous winter of 1890 when starving cows littered the fields, the haybarns were insurance against disaster.

Next to the hay barn and the tack room was a circular corral of almost impossibly thick boards. A snubbing post a foot square was rooted three feet deep in the middle of the corral. The ground was loose dirt six inches deep to minimize the impact when cowboys got bucked off and colts would throw themselves down in protest against the rigors of training. And this was where John D. and his son, Ira, came with their saddlehorses and the Arab colt.

On the way, they had stopped to make a token visit at a picket enclosure that contained the graves of Sarah Hamilton and John D.'s antecedents. John D. had stopped along the way to step out of his saddle and pick a handful of wild daisies. Clutching the fragile flowers in one big work worn hand, John D. placed them carefully in a stone urn in front of Sarah Hamilton's grave. With his head bare, he bent his head and mumbled an inarticulate prayer. "I should come here more often. I'm sorry, Sarah," John D. mumbled. Not wanting to intrude upon the ritual, Ira sat in his saddle and took off his hat and bowed his head.

When they reached the circular training corral, Ira tied the colt to the thick iron ring on the snubbing post, then set about unsaddling his mustang and grooming him, scraping off the sweat and checking his feet to make sure no rocks had wedged themselves in the unprotected frog. John D. did not unsaddle his horse.

"I think I'll check the stock," he said. Ira silently handed him the carbine, and John D. stuffed it into the scabbard. Ira needed no explanation as to his father's real intent. He began his practice of hand-rubbing the Arab colt from hooves to head, then stripped off his shirt and dried the colt with it. The old Indian horse trainer had told him that this was a good way to familiarize the colt with his body smell. If a horse bucked after the intimacy of rubbing, he was not to be trusted. Over the colt's back, Ira watched his father bend down from his saddle to inspect something on the ground.

John D. Hamilton had spotted something, all right. He had cut the rustlers' tracks. His horse moving at a slow walk, he was still bent to one side, looking closely now at whatever he was following. Ira could see that his father had pulled the Winchester out of its scabbard and wedged it between his legs and the bucking rolls of his Morgan horse. Ira watched him as he went on his way until he dipped over a ridge and disappeared from sight. Ira went back to grooming his colt. When he was done, the Arab grew restless.

"He for sure wants to join the others in the big pasture," Ira said to himself. But it was too soon to let the colt out on his own. Instead, Ira turned him loose in the strict confines of the training corral. The colt accepted that halfway measure, but to show his displeasure, he began to roll more than he needed from side to side in the soft dirt of the corral. Ira watched him until he had shaken himself violently to get rid of the dirt that blanketed him, then Ira let himself out and went to the kitchen end of the long cabin.

Pausing at the pump only long enough to splash a token amount of water in the wash basin, he scrubbed his face, dug his fingers into his ears, dried himself on a scrap of towel, and went inside to start dinner. Paper and kindling went into the big stove and the fire was soon roaring.

Ira took no pains with dinner. It had been a long day, and they needed sleep more than food. Slicing thick pieces of bacon off the hanging slab, he laid them side by side in the frying pan. Onions and long slices of potatoes went into the grease. Sourdough bread with a thick crust and a pot of coffee completed preparations for dinner. The scarred little table on the other end of the kitchen was set quickly with tin plates and tin cups, knives and forks.

When the clump of his father's boots sounded on the stoop, Ira served up dinner. Though John D. could make a good stew, the best Ira could provide was bacon and potatoes.

Dinner talk was usually confined to animals and crops and mostly silence, but tonight John D. provided a surprise.

"I hear your Injun friend Cricket has a gift for tracking."

Ira nodded warily and went on chewing his food. When his mind was more at ease, he replied, "Cricket's a wonder, Pa. He can even follow a lizard's tracks."

"Is he nearby?" John D. asked. "Or did he go wandering with the others?"

"He did," Ira said. He was not about to tell his father that the band's destination was the holy ground at Black Rock Springs.

"Shame."

"What did you want him for?"

"I cut some tracks out there beyond the meadow chain," said John D. "About fifty head, traveling together. I can't be sure which direction they are taking. South to Reno country in Nevada or across the Black Rock Desert. Not north to Oregon, because they came from there. Nor east to Mormon country in Utah, because the Mormon battalion would be hot on their trail. If they choose to cross the Black Rock Desert, I would need no help because the tracks left by fifty horses would be like a highway."

"Could they have been a mustang bunch?" said Ira.

"Can't tell. Most was unshod, but a few were wearing shoes."

That meant nothing, the mix between shod and unshod, father and son knew. For many years, ranchers had been turning stallions loose to mix with the mustangs that roamed the hills and flats. Good studs built up the blood of the wild ones, and mustangers often caught and culled potentially good saddle horses out of them. The crossbreeds had an instinct for finding water in unlikely places, and they were predictable.

"Why would rustlers come here?" said Ira, knowing the answer. "Not that many ranches out this way."

"No, there aren't. But there's an Ayrab horse their boss clearly wants." Castrated, he would make some rich rancher's wife a pretty pleasure pony. And earn Hawkeye a pretty sum.

"I'll keep him inside the barn," Ira said with sudden heat. "In a stall."

John D. shook his head. "Not in this hot weather. He'll sicken and die."

"All right, Pa," said Ira. "Can I keep him in the little training corral? He'll be working some with the snubbing post."

"Good," said John D. "He'll be safe there, and the shepherd dog will tell us when something's up."

Ira was not so sure about that. But he also knew the rustlers wouldn't be likely to sneak up that close to men who had no prejudices against using guns against thieves.

"Don't worry," said John D. "Them rustlers can't wait around here forever."

Ira accepted that and went to work training the colt. He started every day with a wash basin holding a generous mixture of oats sweetened with molasses. He knew he was spoiling the colt, but he wanted a friend under him instead of an enemy. While the Arab chewed, Ira began his ritual of rubbing the colt down from head to hoof, paying particular attention to the legs. When the time came, the Arab would be easy to shoe.

The remainder of the training sessions was put over to working the colt with a "lunge line" as some called it, beginning with a proper walk and moving to a trot and a contained lope. The Arab would learn most of what he needed to know when Ira put him to work with cattle.

Then one morning, Ira went out to an empty corral.

The boards were intact and the gates neatly closed, but the Arab was gone. Ira's first reaction was one of disbelief.

Ira did not need to think twice about who had stolen his colt. John D. Hamilton was probably right in his conclusion that the rustlers with fifty-odd head of stolen horses would not wait around just to steal one colt. But John D. had not taken into account that Hawkeye, once his quota had been delivered to some destination, would double back by himself to pick up the first Arab ever seen in Heavenly Valley. He had been serious enough to compete for the colt in the rodeo and then try to steal him from his stall in the livery stable. He had even driven his rustled herd all the way to the Hamilton ranch, waiting for an opportunity. Failing that, he had risked his life coming back to John D.'s ranch alone when he knew he would be met by an armed man and an armed youth, neither of them strangers to guns.

Past the far gate to the training corral, Ira could see the tracks of two horses traveling together. One set would be Hawkeye's saddle horse and the other set, as small as a pony's, was for certain made by Ira's Arab colt.

It took only a little while for Ira to call Calico to the tack room to be tied to the hitching rail, and less time than that to throw a saddle on his back.

With the colt's tracks to mark the way, Ira followed Hawkeye's trail through the sweep of sagebrush to the edge of the

Black Rock Desert. The tracks led plainly out onto the desert, but a riffle of wind was already filling the hoofprints with fine sand. In another hour the tracks would be invisible.

Standing at the dividing line, Ira stared out at more than a hundred miles of sand, pure sand with only a few patches of grass to break it. "A sea of sand, one of the world's seven great deserts," his schoolteacher had called it.

There was no sense going farther. In the first place, he was not equipped for a pursuit. That would be the next order of business. Somewhere out there, Hawkeye was leading the Arab colt to a preordained meeting place. But unknown to Hawkeye, Cricket and Black Rock Tom's band were camped for their ritual pilgrimage to the Indians' holy ground. Ira would have to find the holy ground and the Paiute band if he hoped to recapture his colt and save his own life. There was one consolation. Black-eyed and black-haired Thoma would be somewhere out there, too.

As he sat in his saddle, his hands folded on the horn, staring out over the desert sea, an eddy of wind scooped up a wisp of sand. In the beginning, the wisp was thin as a pencil. Then it began to grow and take shape. Tiny sand particles whirled around, forming a vortex. Ira watched the phenomenon dispassionately. He had seen too many dust devils form to be disturbed by one more. Still, this one seemed to signify something.

Within a few minutes, the dust devil took on a funnel shape that was like a miniature tornado. Ira could have spurred Calico out of its ordained path. Instead he stood his ground, merely pulling up the big bandanna that encircled his neck. The bandanna was silk, not only for warmth but also because a cowboy could see through it when he was enveloped by trail dust.

Ira Hamilton did not consider this trick of nature a bad omen. It was merely the first of the troubles that he would encounter on this journey. Whirling sand and desert debris wrapped around him.

When the dust devil had passed him, Ira pulled down the bandanna, took a deep breath of clean air, and reined Calico in the direction of the Hamilton homestead. It was time to get ready and be on his way to whatever awaited him there in that inscrutable desert.

7

"You may think them thievin' rustlers will be the only en-emies you'll face out there," John D. Hamilton by God said. Standing in the doorway to the tack room, his wide frame almost blocked out the glare of sunlight from outside. He was holding a canvas water bag in one hand. By now only a few drops were forcing their way through the woven can-vas fabric that contained all the water Ira and Calico and a packhorse would start out with, signifying that the water bag was almost cured. "This will be your real enemy," John D. Hamilton said.

Ira looked up with question. He was on his knees on the board floor of the tack room, surrounded by an assortment of leather and canvas packbags, a fire-iron bent into the shape of a hairpin, a small fire-blackened coffeepot, a long-handled frying pan of paper-thin metal to save on weight, ropes and saddlebag harness, and a pile of little flour sacks containing coffee, sugar, salt, flour for baking biscuits, beans, onions, garlic, and a more than adequate supply of cayenne pepper guaranteed to disguise the taste of anything.

"Water? My enemy?" said Ira.

"The lack of it," John D. said. "Out there," waving his hand toward the desert. "Especially in heat that will suck your body dry."

John D.'s lecturing voice went on. "There's a few tricks you should know on how to outsmart the desert. They could save your life."

"Yessir," said Ira obediently.

"The most important thing is to look for mustang trails," said John D. "They go in a straight line, and they go straight to water. Follow them. Sooner or later, they will lead to a water hole. Them wild horses have done a big service for us cowboys by laying those trails in desert or mountain. They've saved our lives, and," he added emphatically, "our saddle horses' lives."

"Well," Ira said. "Calico will be a big help then. He's a mustang."

John D. Hamilton was reluctant ever to acknowledge that Ira's rangy mustang was good for anything. He avoided the trap by changing the subject. "Stay around that water hole for two or three days, until your belly, your skin, and your animals are soaked with water. Then move on."

"Yessir," Ira said with impatience. He wasted no time in argument.

"Remember not to get too far from the edge of the sage-brush flats. If it rains and you are out on the Black Rock, the desert will turn into quicksand in an hour, and you'll be there for good. Get the hell to sagebrush and solid ground."

John D. Hamilton had been drumming Ira full of advice about his pursuit of Hawkeye's rustlers, while odds and ends began to be tucked away in the saddlebags, including a burlap sack partially filled with barley for the horses. When Ira appeared impatient again, John D. said, "Don't be too sparing on the barley. Your horses will need all the strength they can get. There's damned little grass in a true desert."

His father was right about that. Ira had learned a few lessons in the one and only foray he had made into the Black Rock with Cricket and Black Rock Tom. "I know that, Pa," said Ira. "I saw it for myself a long time back."

"How did that come to be?" John D. demanded.

"I went out there once with Black Rock Tom and Cricket."

"Playin' Injun," said John D. with contempt. "I should have known. Is this where Cricket was when I needed him to follow rustler tracks?"

Ira did not respond. No need, when the answer was obvious.

"The ground cloth is to keep the cold from your back," said John D. "And the wool blanket to keep you warm. People think the desert is hot. At night, you can freeze out there. Melt in the day, freeze in the night. It's a good thing to remember."

Ira nodded in assent. He had learned that lesson, too, on the horseback trip with Black Rock Tom and Cricket. His estimation of his father's knowledge of the wilderness went up appreciably.

"Don't forget there's four of them rustlers and one of you," warned John D. "That can't make for a fair fight." John D.'s voice dropped. "Be careful, son."

57

It was the first time Ira had heard that note of concern in his father's voice. "If I find Cricket, the odds will even up some."

"Some don't mean enough," said John D. "Those are gun slicks out there. I wish you would change your mind." The appeal was torn from John D. Hamilton in a tone that said it would be the only time in his life he would ask anything of his son.

If Ira bowed his head, it would spell out a shame he could not bear. "I can't, Pa," he said. "No more than if you were me in my time and trouble." He could not run to Papa like a boy. He was a man now.

Ira scrambled to his feet in the tangle of rope and leather spread out around the saddlebags. A flurry of hay dust flew up and powdered the faces of both father and son. Afterwards, when the tangle had untangled and the dust had settled, Ira swore to himself it was the dust that misted his father's eyes for a solitary instant.

8

On his third day out, Ira nearly lost his life. In less than a minute, the sand beneath him and his horse had become a morass that caught at their feet and hooves. They were only a hundred yards from the safety of sagebrush land, but it might have been five miles. They were caught in a sudden summer squall. Ira raised his face to the rain and screamed, "But Pa, I didn't go far out. See for yourself. I minded you."

For the first time since he had captured the mustang, Ira dug his spurs deep into Calico's flanks, so deep that he could look down and see his spur points drawing blood. "I won't make it, I won't make it," he cried. Then suddenly, a barrier of rocks appeared as if by magic to his right and he remembered them for what they were, a pockmarked promontory that projected out into the desert. In the late light they were almost purple hued. Calico stumbled forward. In a flash of memory from his first trip into the Black Rock, Ira remembered seeing the long line of pockmarked rocks, the dark opening of a cave and the rocky ledge that covered it. Ira ducked his head and rode underneath the rock shelf that would shelter him and his horses from the deluge. He found himself on a bed of volcanic sand with solid substance under it. And it was dry! When he knew he and his animals were safe for sure, he swung out of the saddle and bent down to see the damage his spurs had done to Calico. He pressed his hand against the horse's flank. It came away red, but the bleeding had already stopped. Light was fading, and he looked about him to determine how big a cave he had stumbled into. He was in a rock shelter with a low ceiling and just enough room to accommodate him and his two horses.

In one corner crevice, there was a sizable pile of twigs and branches left by pioneers who carried fuel with them and leaves blown in from the sagebrush desert. They served only to remind Ira that he was drenched through and beginning to shiver. He must dry himself before he chilled. From an inner shirt pocket he pulled out a Prince Albert tobacco can stuffed with thick lucifer matches. Carefully so as not to wet his supply, he eased out one single match and struck it against the rock wall. The match flared, and he touched it to the base of the driest pile of leaves he had gathered. There was an uncertain moment when the leaves smoked more than burned, and then they burst into flame.

Even more carefully, Ira fed the smallest twigs he had gathered and crisscrossed them on his tinder. Larger twigs and dry branches joined the flames. A reassuring warmth flowed into the rock shelter. Garment by garment, Ira stripped off his clothes and held jacket and jerkin and shirt to the flow of heat. In a few minutes, the shelter began to gather warmth, and Ira finished drying himself. He sniffed deeply, but not too much smoke had gathered in the shelter. It was streaming upwards into a knifelike fissure that pierced the ceiling of the rock cavern. Man and animals were safe. Ira flopped back on the warm sand and went to sleep.

When Ira awoke, he could not be sure whether he had been dreaming. All he knew for certain was that he was dry and warm and lying on his back in a bed of black crystal sand. His gaze was fixed on an image barely an arm's length above his face. If he reached out his hand, he could touch the white outline of the horned ram's visage that looked down on him. It resembled a child's drawing of a mountain goat with curving horns. But he knew for an absolute fact that he dare not succumb to the temptation to trace the deep white lines etched in the rock that was roof to his prone figure. If he did, something of the unknown would wreak its vengeance upon him.

When his memory began functioning again, he remembered the ordeal he had been through—the floundering in the morass that the Black Rock Desert had become with the cloudburst of unexpected rain, the miracle of the cave he had fought his way into, the wet and freezing cold, the life-giving warmth of the fire in the chimneylike crevice, and finally, the collapse of utter weariness into the bed of sand. Remembering the fire, he realized now that similar fires had been built in the crevice for God knows how long a time. It was a small leap to the accompanying knowledge that the horned white ram above him had been etched into the rock by the first men the shamans of Black Rock Tom's band spoke about in hushed and reverent tones. The temptation to laugh at his imaginings was too close for comfort. It was supplanted by a desire to escape from the cave inhabited by the ancients and get out into the desert sun and endless sweeps of open land and be on his way.

An hour under the searing sun cleansed Ira of his apparitions, and he shaded his eyes to stare into the never-ending distance in search of the landmark Black Rock Tom had told him to watch for—the black opalized pinnacle called Black Rock. It had served as landmark for everyone from the first Indian hunting parties, white explorers who had left their mark on the rock walls beside the trail to Oregon, pioneers, prospectors and the first cowmen seeking a place to settle, and now him.

The realization that he was all alone in a waterless land did not come home to Ira until the third day without water. When John D. Hamilton's water bag was drained dry, Ira began to know fear. By then, his tongue had begun to swell in his mouth and those of Calico and the packhorse had started to turn black.

Finally, it was Calico, the unpretty and unwanted mustang, who would save their lives. The gentle packhorse was the first to show signs of going loco. It began when he started pawing the ground as if to dig down to water. Then his nostrils closed until he was snorting and gasping painfully for air. Ira watched until he could tolerate it no longer. The suffering animal had to be put out of his misery. Stepping out of the saddle, Ira unsheathed the Winchester, levered a cartridge into the breech and took aim. His control of gun and eye had been worsened by the debilitating thirst so that he could not chance a free-standing shot. Instead, he rested the elbow of his left arm on the seat of his saddle and again took aim. The front sight was notched between the packhorse's eyes, but Ira could not hold it there. If he fired, the best he could hope for would be a wounding shot that would only serve to worsen the packhorse's misery. Calico saved Ira the agony of a decision by tossing his head as if he were just plain mad at the ways of humans. He burst into a gallop at right angles to the direction they had been traveling.

Running Calico down on foot was hopeless, and Ira saved his remaining breath for shouting at his runaway horse. Calico must have been nearly out of earshot when finally he seemed to hear Ira's voice for the first time. He slowed to a lope, stopped in indecision, and then trotted reluctantly back to Ira. Giving Calico no time to change his mind, Ira pulled himself into the saddle.

Once in the saddle, Ira took it for granted he had control of the situation. He was wrong again. Ignoring the punishing bit, Calico turned back in the direction he had been traveling and broke into a run. Ira saw he was following an old creek bed that had gone dry. The farther Calico ran, Ira could feel the sand beneath the mustang's hooves growing spongy. When Calico's hooves splashed water, Ira felt his heart expand with gratitude.

Calico found his own destination, a pool of muddy water deep enough to drink by sucking through the filter of his teeth. It was only when Calico stopped sucking water that Ira stepped cautiously out of the stirrup and dropped to his knees in the mud. Following Calico's example, he put his mouth in the mud and began sucking water. Strength returned to his body as his weakened limbs sucked up moisture. It was only when he could lift himself into the security of the saddle that he raised his eyes and looked back to see where the creek had come from. He looked back once before he went on to see what had become of the packhorse. He was lying unmoving on the sand. Ira retraced his steps to take what he could carry on Calico.

When he faced forward again, Ira did not accept what he was seeing. It was not a question of belief that grass-filled meadows and a shining creek could exist in this desolate region. It was a matter of trust in what he was seeing. In the desert he had traversed, he had been deceived twice, pursuing what he swore were shimmering lakes lined with tall trees. But when he got to where he thought lake and trees were, he realized that they did not exist. They were what the old prospectors who had crossed the Black Rock Desert called mirages, tricks that desert glare would play on a man.

When the sound of Calico's teeth tearing at long grass reached his ears, Ira began to believe that *this* was not a mirage. He and Calico were penetrating the beginning of a sweep of rich green pastures. As if to give credence to what he was seeing, Ira smelled campfire smoke, saw a conical prospector's tent and a man standing in front of it, waving an honest-to-goodness shirt.

9

"You didn't miss connecting up with Hawkeye and his boys by much," the old man said. "A week maybe. It'll take him another week, I figure, to move that many hosses to the Running Iron spread. That's home base for rustled stock in these parts, as you must know."

Ira didn't know. "That's a funny name for a ranch."

The old man slapped his leg. "It's funnier than you think," he guffawed. "Do you know what a running iron is? It's range lingo for a branding iron rustlers use to change a real brand. The name fits, when you consider the Running Iron is one of the biggest rustling operations in the whole durned West. If you was a cattle outfit and you needed a cavvy of fifty or a hundred horses in a hurry, you would just put in an order with old man Carpenter, and he would deliver them hosses right to your doorstep. Same goes for rodeo stock. What you need, the Running Iron has. By the time the hosses have crossed this far on the Black Rock Desert, they're hungry and thirsty. They couldn't make it to the Running Iron without feeding up, drinking up, and resting up. Here. Their only other way to make it is reaching Black Rock Springs, which is occupied by Black Rock Tom and his Paiutes. That would be like dropping in to visit a nest full of rattlesnakes, with the meanest rattlesnake of all barring their way.

"Is this your grass?"

"Finders keepers," the old man cackled. "I found it, and I claim it. Nobody argues that."

Ira shook his head in wonderment. "It's the best kept secret in the West. I won't tell. Hawkeye stops here regular?"

"Regular as hell," the old man said. "This is the halfway rest stop if he expects to reach the home base of Running Iron with hosses that Carpenter would pay a nickel for."

"Will Hawkeye be back this way?"

The old man shook his wattles. There was practically no flesh on his bones except for the wattles under his chin. He was the stringiest man Ira had ever seen, with a long face grooved with wrinkles as deep as ravines, blue eyes shot with red veins, and a moustache that resembled straw jutting out sideways from his nostrils. The old man insisted that he be called Old-Timer "because it's so," he said. "I'm older than the hills I spent my life digging into. Without luck," he added, "until I got my fortune finding grass to sell to rustlers."

The question had been building up in Ira's mind from the moment he had found out about the old man's arrangement with the rustlers. "Did Hawkeye have some extra-special horses this time around?"

"As a matter of fact, he did," said the old man. "He had a colt he said was an Ayrab. Prettiest little animal I ever seen. Hawkeye treated him like a baby. Said he had a special place for that little beauty. I figure he's being saved for some rich rancher's wife."

The old man interrupted his chatter when he stood up to peer into the distance. "Well, speak of the devil and what do you get? It has to be Hawkeye and one of his boys and two packhorses, with provisions to keep me going." The old man peered more intensely. "They ain't paying a social call. They got their rifles out." The old man regarded Ira with suspicion now. "If you got troubles with Hawkeye, keep me out of it."

Ira swung into the saddle and reined Calico in the direction of the Black Rock Desert. When he judged enough time had passed to show he was not intimidated, he eased the Winchester out of its boot and rested its butt against his thigh, pointedly ignoring the rustlers. Out of the corner of his eye, Ira saw Hawkeye saying something to his partner. "They got no call to shoot me," he thought to himself. "And they darned well won't do it with the old man looking on. If they decide to follow me, I will lead them into that rattlesnake nest the old man had on his mind, and I will personally introduce him to the meanest rattlesnake of all, Black Rock Tom."

Hawkeye and his friend were talking volubly to the old man. It did not need much foresight to guess what they were talking about. Suddenly, Hawkeye shouted across the intervening space, "I seen you before! You ain't fooling me!"

"And you're liable to see me again!" Ira shouted. He was sure his voice had not carried to Hawkeye, but it didn't matter. "Just as well keep my whereabouts a secret until I need to make them known."

10

Ira had been following the path between the two wagon-wheel ruts for an hour before it occurred to him he was traveling the old Emigrant Trail. The path between the ruts had been scraped clear, and the ruts carved by the iron wheel rims of fifty years ago were nearly a foot deep. Ira's grandparents—father and mother to John D. Hamilton—had been among the first pioneers to travel this trail, and when Ira realized that, he knew wonderment at what the pioneers had overcome.

The debris of the pioneers littered the sides of the Emigrant Trail—rusted iron rims of giant size, wooden wheel spokes, discarded utensils worn out beyond saving, splintered pieces of furniture too fragile to survive the trip West, rotted scraps of once-sturdy harness—discards all.

Here and there away from the trail were the holes dug in

fruitless probings for water, and every once in a while, a hole that was still bubbling clear and cold water that had sated oxen and horses and pioneers until the water casks were again empty and a new hole was dug in another promising place.

The trail wound through a treacherous terrain of springs so hot that they spewed miniature geysers of boiling water. Where the geysers had cut basins, their bottoms were filled with the whitened bones of oxen and horses too driven by thirst to avoid the hot springs. Boiling water had literally scalded flesh and hair away.

In another plain through which the wagons had carved their way, there was a forest of grass tufts whose roots had been exposed by the ceaseless wind that swept away tiny particles of sand to the accompaniment of moaning music that was unsettling to a man's senses and soul. Sometimes the main trail veered crazily away from its proven route and went twisting through the sagebrush wilderness. Ira knew what that meant. His grandfather had spun tales of night fog descending upon the wagon train, erasing direction on all sides. It had almost happened to Ira before he remembered what his grandfather told him about being trapped and blinded by fog until someone in the train remembered hearing how earlier pioneers had saved themselves. Ira spurred Calico right to the top of the highest hill he could see, until he was above the fog blanket and could see the faithful landmark of the opalized Black Rock looming in the distance. The pioneers and Ira, too, stayed on their high perches until the desert sun had burned away the fog blanket and they could go on their way.

When the Winchester got to be a bother to carry with its barrel canted upwards, Ira stuffed it back into its boot. Still, he could not rid himself of the feeling that he was being followed. It was a strange sensation, because danger did and did not accompany it. But he could not chance trusting his instincts all the way. When the tingling began to play up and down his spine, he unsheathed and upended the Winchester and carried it on the ready.

Slowly but unerringly, Ira was nearing the Black Rock landmark where he would find the big spring and—he hoped—the Paiute band before their summer pilgrimage to holy ground and the oasis in the desert was ended and they returned home to Heavenly Valley.

It was at a moment when he felt most secure with anticipation of the reunion with the Paiute band that he abandoned precaution and lingered too long in the twilight on the rim of a desert hill. He felt the slamming impact of the bullet high on his back before he heard the echo of the shot. He pitched forward off his saddle and landed face down on the gravel-grained earth.

As he lay there, Calico turned and came back to him, his muzzle and ears pointed angrily in the direction from which the shot had come. The last sound Ira heard before he slipped into unconsciousness made no sense at all. There was a flurry of shots that sounded exactly like the shot that had downed him, and the piercing battle cry of a warrior from Black Rock Tom's Paiute band.

11

"Goddamit! You ain't gonna die on me until you see what I got waiting."

Ira put his one good hand on Cricket's chest and shoved. "Leave me alone!" he cried. "I'm hurting enough without you roughing me up." Then his resistance gave way to weakness, and he collapsed backwards into a basket of intertwined arms. Two Paiute braves wedged their arms under Ira's armpits, and two more sets of arms were clasped behind his knees. Cricket provided the last support to the makeshift chair by grabbing a handful of Ira's straw-blond hair, none too gently, to keep his head from flopping. Blood was pouring down the back of Ira's shirt, but no one seemed to think it was important.

"You gonna like this," Cricket said gleefully. "But this

fellow didn't like what happened to him. Hawkeye called him Curt. He won't need a name now."

Ira said nothing. There was a suspicious smell of sulfuric fumes clinging to Cricket.

"What did you do with him?"

"Made him hurt a little," said Cricket. "But it didn't last long."

"How did you kill him?"

"None of your business," said Cricket. "He's the one who shot you. He paid for it."

"Where did you bury him?" asked Ira.

"I show you," said Cricket and led the way for Ira and his carriers through a maze of basins filled with boiling water. Sulfuric fumes gagged Ira as they followed Cricket. Each of the basins held its particular collection of whitened bones—pioneers' oxen that had probably gone mad for water, lizards and birds, and every once in a while, the unmistakable skeleton of a human. Cricket pointed to one basin in particular. "There's the bones of the son-of-a-bitch who shot you in the back. The way he's falling apart, nobody will know a week from now who he was."

"How did you catch him?"

"We ran him into the boulders," said Cricket. "He was a fighter. When his horse went down, he kept shooting from behind rocks. I climbed up the back way, hanging on like a lizard, and jumped him when he wasn't looking." Cricket patted the blunt edge of his tomahawk. "Knocked him out, and we roped his hands and feet and dragged him here to the ovens. He was a pretty good yeller, too, when that hot clay started dropping on him and burning its way through." Cricket scowled. "That Hawkeye bastard was a tricky one. He outran us all through the boulders. He got away."

"We know where he went to," said Ira.

"Running Iron spread," said Cricket. "That's where we go next. When you're up to it."

"I'm up to it now."

"No," said Cricket. "You lost a lot of blood. You look like hell. Sure as anything, that shot in your back is going to give you a fever."

"I guess you're right."

"My father's shaman is right. He's the doctor. I sent one of my friends back to Black Rock Tom. He talked to the shaman, and the shaman told him what to expect and how to cure it. By this time tomorrow, you'll be on your back in the shaman's special tent, drinking his medicine and listening to his medicine, and—" Cricket grinned, "chewing his peyote and having good dreams."

"I won't eat any shaman's mess of lizards and snakes," Ira said.

"You won't have to," said Cricket. "I'll hunt your meat for you and a woman will cook it just the way you like it. I've got someone to nurse you until you get well."

"Your mother?"

"My sister, Thoma."

When finally the fever broke, Ira lay prone and unmoving on the deerskin robe that had served as his bed for a dozen days. His gaze was fixed on the smoke hole at the top of the shaman's head. Day and night, night and day, the smoke hole had been the center of his existence, spinning and whirling, filled with sun and stars, blinding colors and violent images. Unceasing sound had accompanied the colors and images, the pulsating beat of drums, the pounding of moccasined feet on the moist earth, the eerie chanting of the shaman's voice, his eyes moving in concentric circles, and the incessant, rhythmic, dry-as-death rattle of pebbles encased in dried gourds.

Sight and sound were interspersed by the sensation of touch—the porcelain fingers of the shaman's fragile hands rubbing sacred signs into Ira's forehead and reaching behind him to pass his palm over the hole the rustler's bullet had made. The first duty the shaman had performed when Ira was laid on his face in the lodge was to wash away the debris that was threatening to infect the wound. The shaman had carefully pulled shreds of Ira's shirt out of the crater the bullet had made. Then he set his mouth to encircle the bullet hole and sucked out everything alien that clung there. Ira had been fortunate that his blood flowed freely, helping to wash out the debris. The shaman's trained lips sucked mouthful after mouthful of clotted blood out of the wound. His lungs were so powerful that he almost went too far, starting a hemorrhage that bled as freely as the bullet wound itself. When he realized he was going too far, the shaman reached into a leather pouch and took out feathery down taken from an eagle's breast and packed it into the hole. The network of fibers stemmed the flow of blood. Still guarding against infection, the shaman mixed the eagle down with powder made from a blue-belly lizard that had been boiled, pounded to a jelly, and let dry in the sun. Then came a succession of touching hands, Black Rock Tom's hard-as-leather palms touching Ira's cheeks and ordering him to get well, Cricket pulling at his hair. But most often, Thoma holding up his head with one hand and tipping a gourd filled with healing broth of skunk cabbage to fight off infection. And finally, at the end of a siege of fever, Thoma's cool palms stroking his temples and saying without words that she loved him.

On the day Ira awakened with the dawn captured in the smoke hole, they all knew that he would not die, but get well. The time of recuperation set in.

It was in this time that the three young friends began to talk about what still seemed an impossibility, that Ira and Thoma could actually live as man and wife.

Knowing what a father must be feeling when his son's life was in doubt, Black Rock Tom sent a messenger to John D. Hamilton by God telling him that his son was still alive, that he had been shot by rustlers in the Black Rock Desert, that he had been treated by an Indian medicine man and was going to get well.

Ira laughed and Cricket read his mind. "Your Injun hatin' father would never let you live on his land with an Injun wife."

"Maybe. Maybe not. We'll see."

"Those milk-white women with long noses would call her a dirty squaw . . ."

Thoma's lynx eyes flashed with fury. "If one does, I'll cut off her tits."

For the rest of his lifetime, Ira would remember the healing time as one of a dream in which the air that surrounded him and Thoma was filled with a golden haze. They would awaken after a night of love and dive soundlessly into the warm waters of the pool, swim until Ira's strength waned, float on their backs until they were sated with water, and sleep in sun and sand until Ira was restored.

In these times, Ira devoured sleep like a hungry lion replenishing itself in the aftermath of an exhausting hunt.

Three deerskins cured and stretched were unrolled in the afternoon shade, and they would while away hours shaping obsidian into small, razor-edged arrow points for birds and small game, larger points for deer and antelope, and wicked projectile heads for wildcat and cougar whose skins would become sleeping robes.

At dusk, Cricket would join them at their campfire for talk and the last meal of the day. Afterwards, they made their way to the dancing ground. While Cricket danced war dances with the other young braves, Ira and Thoma watched the bronzed skins become glistening with sweat and joined in the singing until they could slip away unnoticed. At the pool's edge, they would shed their clothes and dive again into Black Rock Spring to swim with long relaxing strokes in the moonlight and, finally, float effortlessly on their backs through the steam that rose from the warm water into the chilly night air.

When the sound of the dancing diminished to nothing, they crept like shadows to their tent and made love. It was not the passionate predatory love they knew in their court-ship, but languorous, deepening love of absolute bonding.

Then came the time when Ira and Cricket palavered with Black Rock Tom, mapping their passage through Running Iron country, what dangers they could expect and prepar-ing themselves for what was to come.

Then one night, Ira leaned over Thoma and kissed her eyes. She closed her eyes and whispered good-bye. Sound-lessly, Ira left their tent and went to meet Cricket at their appointed place. They armed themselves and daubed their faces with the paint the shaman had decreed them for brav-ery and safe passage.

12

The hawk flew up into the wind and hovered there, wings flat and unwavering, caught and immobilized where the speed of the oncoming wind equaled his wing speed. Then, tilting his wings, he banked into the wind stream that carried him down and away with incredible speed. In a matter of seconds, he had shot the course of the longest valley Ira and Cricket had ever seen. It was at least a hundred miles long, and flat, and blanketed with gray-green sagebrush hugging the ground like a carpet.

At first sight, the wide valley seemed as though it would be easy to cross even at a contained trot. Ira and Cricket were to learn differently.

On the far horizon, there was a mountain range of sharply defined angles and bare sharp peaks. From where they sat their horses there was not a tree to be seen, which meant there would be no semblance of shade for days to come.

Ira and Cricket were three days into the crossing when they smelled the smoke of a cooking fire. When distance allowed, they saw a chuck wagon and cowboys sprawled around it eating a lunch of beans and bacon out of battered tin plates. For miles ahead, steers and calves, moving along in no particular hurry, dotted the landscape. It was a cattle roundup instead of rustlers, but still they approached it with apprehension.

A bearded cowboy with a tall crowned hat and a holstered pistol met them. "You're a little on the young side for rustlers," he said.

Ira said angrily, "We're not rustlers. We're looking for the Running Iron spread."

"Cool down, son," said the bearded cowboy. "Hereabouts, the only riders on Running Iron ground are rustlers."

"Then we're on the right track," said Ira to Cricket. To the bearded cowboy, he said, "*They* stole my horse."

"Hey, I seen you before," said another cowboy. "Ain't you the one who rode old Thunder out at the Heavenly Valley rodeo? Such a ride I never seen."

The bearded cowboy shed his hostility. "Apologies. Grab some beans and bacon and give your horses a breather." He pointed toward the cast iron Dutch oven resting on a fire iron. "What in hell are you doing so far away from home? Running Iron land ain't exactly safe. You could get yourself shot by one of them no-goods who call this territory home."

"He's already been shot," Cricket announced. "In the back."

The bearded cowboy whistled. "And you're coming back for more? I hope you got friends to back you up."

"Not friends," said Cricket. "Our families."

"And who might they be?" the bearded cowboy said skeptically.

"His father is John D. Hamilton by God. Mine is Black Rock Tom."

The bearded cowboy did not conceal his being impressed. "That's a pair to draw to. I wouldn't want to be the man who stole your horse. Call me Ben Jonson."

"Hawkeye," said the cowboy who had admired Ira's ride. "I remember hearing now. He stole this young cowboy's prize for winning the bronc busting—a colt nobody seen the likes of before. *Ayrab,* they said he was. Prettiest horse I ever saw."

"That's all well and good," said the bearded cowboy. "But the bastard who stole him is just about the meanest man there ever was. You're going to need your pas and maybe then some to stand him off."

"We'll see about that."

"Unless I miss my guess, you don't even know where he's holed up."

"We'll find him."

"That I doubt," said the bearded cowboy. "I'll tell you what I'll do. Point you to the Running Iron from close up. From then on, you're on your own. I owe you that much for calling you a rustler."

The bearded cowboy, Ben Jonson, was as good as his word. By late afternoon, he had led Ira and Cricket to a rocky knoll overlooking the Running Iron ranch.

There didn't seem to be anything the Running Iron lacked. Central to it was a three-story white frame ranch house with a porch that almost encircled the first floor. Windows were paned and curtained, reflecting the presence of Carpenter's wife and daughters. Next to the big house was the cookhouse, surrounded by a dozen small buildings that housed the dairy, smokehouse, blacksmith shop, harness shop, and a bunkhouse.

"Old man Carpenter's not hurting for money," said Ben Jonson. "A rustling outfit this big never does. I know the foreman," he said, "but that don't make me a rustler," he added, grinning at Ira. "He and I rodeoed together a long time back. He don't owe me no favors, but our being rodeoers gives me the opening to ask him if Hawkeye is holed up here and if he's got the little Ayrab hid away somewhere. If he says yes, you offer to buy the horse. No rough stuff. Rustlers or not, these people are our neighbors. I don't want to start a feud. Is that clear?"

"It is," said Ira.

Next morning, Ben Jonson led Ira and Cricket as far as the vantage point overlooking the ranch. "If that Ayrab is anywhere, it will be in one of those inside pens. If Hawkeye spooks when he hears I've talked to old man Carpenter, he'll try to sneak the Ayrab out the back way. You can spot him from here."

Ben Jonson left them and rode alone down to the ranch. Ira and Cricket concealed themselves behind a stand of rocks overlooking the ranch.

"We do what Ben Jonson says," said Cricket. "But if Hawkeye tries to sneak out, I say we got the right to stop him any way we can. Rough stuff or not. Hell with any bargain."

"I'm not sure," said Ira.

"I am," said Cricket. "They tried to kill you. Isn't that proof enough not to trust them?"

"Let's wait and see."

"Oh, shit! What does it take to show you a snake?"

Their dilemma solved itself. As they watched, Ben Jonson came out of the ranch house and mounted his horse. There was no hesitancy in his movements as he spurred his horse into a trot and headed in their direction.

"Look!" said Cricket. "There's all the proof you need." He jabbed his finger at the inside pens, where a rider and two horses were caught up in a flurry of movement. The gate to the open country flew open and Hawkeye emerged, unmistakable in black from hat to boots. Spurring his horse and leading another, a pearl-gray colt, he was wasting no time getting away.

"Ayrab!" exclaimed Ira.

13

"Hold on!" Ben Jonson shouted, reining in his horse on the knoll where Ira and Cricket were waiting impatiently.

"Hawkeye's got friends out there," said Ben Jonson. "They'll fill you full of holes if you make a grab for him."

"What happened down there with Hawkeye and old man Carpenter?" Ira cried.

"The old man told Hawkeye he had to give your horse back," said Ben Jonson. "He doesn't want to lock horns with your pa, and especially not with Black Rock Tom."

"How did Hawkeye take that?" said Ira.

"You're seeing how he took it," said Ben Jonson. "He walked out in a huff, telling old man Carpenter he was starting an operation of his own. That's where he's heading now."

"And we're supposed to take it laying down?" Cricket

cried. "Come on, white brother. Let's get going before Hawk-eye and Ayrab are out of sight."

Ben Jonson held up his hands. "I'm telling you, hold on. Use your heads for something other than to put your hats on. Will you listen now?"

"Make it quick," said Ira.

"Watch it, son," said Ben Jonson in a cold voice. He waited, but was met only with silence. "Hawkeye and his boys are holed up somewhere close to town," he went on. "Winnemucca is his hangout. That's the place where he's rounding up money and cowboys for his go at rustling. I got a friend there who's heard his empty talk. Wait until dark, and you can find out what you need to know from him. He's a Basque, and the Basques don't hold with steal-ing. Never have."

"Would he take us out to Hawkeye's hideout?" said Ira. "For sure, that's where Ayrab will be."

"That's between him and you. He's an independent sort. He makes up his own mind."

Ben Jonson swung down off his horse. Ira and Cricket did the same. They hunched down in a group while Ben Jonson told them what he felt they needed to know.

Winnemucca was the biggest town either Ira or Cricket had ever seen. Ben Jonson had told them there were actually a thousand people living in the small frame houses that lined the back streets, shaded by cottonwood trees and long rows of sentinel poplars. There were another hundred or so men on the go, mostly salesmen and stock buyers renting rooms in two-and three-story hotels that offered an iron bed, a mattress and one blanket, a wash stand with a crockery basin, soap, and a scrap of a towel. The rest of the male population stayed in boardinghouses catering to workers in the railroad stockyards.

Livestock was Winnemucca's reason for existence. Cattlemen and sheepmen drove calves and lambs from the open range to the stockyards, made their deals with buyers, paid off their buckaroos and sheepherders in cash, paid their standing bills at the stores and shops, and deposited the rest in the Nevada Bank of Commerce—a stone-and-pillared edifice that was Winnemucca's seal of standing as a real town.

On the outskirts of town were two houses with red lanterns that burned at night, firmly establishing Winnemucca's status as a town to be taken seriously. The whorehouses, legal under Nevada law, catered mostly to the needs of a constant stream of cowboys, sheepherders, and working men and doubled as a stopping-off place for an after-work drink for some of the town's businessmen.

As Ben Jonson had instructed them, Ira and Cricket rode into town at dusk, walking their horses unobtrusively down the main road through the heart of town. Their destination was the saloon that, with the coming of night, was showing signs of activity. The hitching rail was filling up, and two dusty buckaroos with pistols in their belts were trading stories. Ira reined back to take a closer look at the black horse he would be hitching up next to.

A pair of chaps had been slung over the saddle of the horse Ira was eyeing. They were black and winged, and the wings were studded with a poker hand—spade, heart, club, and diamond. Ira looked at Cricket, and Cricket nodded in understanding. The poker-hand chaps were the ones Hawkeye had been wearing at the Fourth of July parade in Heavenly Valley.

Cricket and Ira took their time hitching their horses, talking in low tones.

"Ben Jonson didn't tell us to expect this," said Ira. "Looks like our friend's inside."

Cricket was not troubled. "All the better."

"Why?"

"When he leaves, we leave with him"

"What if he kicks up a fuss?"

In answer, Cricket eased his revolver out of its holster and checked the load. "Let's be ready for him."

Cricket turned his back on Ira as if to check his saddle. When he lifted his stirrup flap, Ira saw for the first time that Cricket's scabbard contained a short powerful bow and a thin quiver of arrows. "What the hell?" Ira asks.

"Indian man. Indian way."

Ira shook his head. "And dead Indian, for killing a white man."

"It won't be the first time."

"That's the old days."

Ira shut off whatever he was going to say. Instead, he led the way toward the saloon's high doors.

Two signs flanked the doors. One said simply, WINNE-MUCCA SALOON. A longer sign beneath it said, THIS IS GOD'S COUNTRY. DON'T RIDE THROUGH IT LIKE HELL.

Green-felt card tables with hanging lamps dominated the room. Only part of them had games going. They would fill up later when whiskey had dulled judgment and egged on courage. So soon after work, the long bar was filling up with men whose duties for the day were done.

Ira stepped through the door and stopped. He had almost collided with the sinewy, black-garbed figure of Hawkeye.

Hawkeye was the first to recover. "What in hell are you

doing *here*? The hotshot bronc rider from Heavenly Valley. Jesus Christ, don't you ever give up?"

Ira had been anticipating this face-to-face encounter with doubts about his own reaction. His gaze level with Hawkeye's, he was surprised that his fear had been displaced. This sinewy outlaw with all the trappings of a gunfighter did not frighten him. He was a man to be taken seriously, but not to the point of being paralyzed in his presence.

"I'm not giving up until I get my horse back."

If Hawkeye were considering a showdown or a shoot-out, he gave up the idea. This encounter ended much like Hawkeye's exchange with John D. Hamilton by God. Ira shouldered his way past Hawkeye and made for the bar. It was almost a reckless thing to do. Hawkeye's hand dropped to his gun. Cricket stepped between him and the retreating figure of Ira. The encounter was over, at least for the time being.

Someone was waving from the end of the bar.

Ben Jonson's friend was named Marcelino. He was lean and dark and intense, and from the first moment of their meeting, Ira knew he was being judged. "Ben says Hawkeye stole your horse."

"He did. I won him at the Heavenly Valley Fourth of July rodeo."

"How did you know he was here in Winnemucca country?"

"We followed him here. Across the Black Rock Desert and the long valley."

Marcelino made a whistling sound with his mouth. "He must be worth a bundle to bring you this far."

"I don't know what he's worth, and I don't care. He's just my horse."

"Best reason of all," said Marcelino. "What do you want from me?"

"We're not asking you to get involved," said Ira. "This is our trouble, not yours. We just want to know where Hawkeye is holed up."

Marcelino was silent, making up his mind. "Him and his buddies and their stolen goods are holed up near my family's sheep ranch. About five cowboys and fifty horses. Word is that Hawkeye's going into the rustling business on his own."

Ira swept the barroom with his gaze. Nobody seemed to be interested in his talking to Marcelino.

"Looking for someone?" said Marcelino.

"No, just making sure we're not getting you into trouble on our account."

"Don't worry about it. No trouble here that my brothers and me can't handle." He finished his drink and stood up. "Time to go anyway. I got a buckboard out in back with provisions for the ranch. Meet you outside."

They followed a well-worn trail through sagebrush and shad scale trampled down by horses, sheep, and cattle. When they reached a desert sort of crossroads, Marcelino pulled back on his reins and waited for Ira and Cricket to catch up with him.

"Okay, here's where we part company," he said. "I take the trail to my ranch, and you go cross country from here. It'll take you about an hour to reach the pass where you can look down and see Hawkeye's ranch. Hawkeye and his buddies will be in an old cabin at the bottom of the hollow. You can spot it by window light and moonlight shining off creek water running through the ranch. They'll all be inside and, with luck, pretty well drunked up by this time. Still, don't take a chance on their knowing you're about. Don't run your horses. Walk them."

"Where will their horse herd be?" asked Cricket.

"In a big corral that touches on the creek," said Marcelino. "About fifty head, I would guess."

"Have you seen my little Ayrab?"

"Hawkeye keeps him in a little corral next to the cabin. He's taking no chances, so watch your step," said Marcelino. "These guys are gun boys, and they can shoot straight, if all their target practice means anything. Sounds like a small war down there when they're target shooting."

Marcelino paused. "I don't want to spook you, but if you get shot, make it back here and down this trail to our sheep ranch. We'll patch you up best we can."

Ira swallowed. "We'll try to spare you the bother. We'll make it up to you down the line."

Marcelino clucked his tongue and flipped his reins. The buckboard disappeared into the darkness.

Ira and Cricket stood their horses in silence, undecided about what to do next.

"Well," sighed Cricket. "Let's do what we came to do. No backing down now, brother."

Ira led the way, walking Calico at a slow, steady pace. "We go in together," he said. "No splitting up."

The sound of voices raised in drunken tones came sooner than they expected. Cricket dismounted, handed his reins to Ira, and crept forward into the darkness. When his movement stopped, Ira knew that he was watching the situation below.

When Cricket had made his way back, he remained dismounted. "We better go on foot."

"What's the layout?"

"Just about like Marcelino said. I'd feel better if there was less of them and more of us."

"Could you see Ayrab or Hawkeye?"

"I made out the little corral. There was a horse inside, but I couldn't tell if it was Ayrab."

"Hawkeye?"

"I saw him good. He stepped out on the porch to piss. He looked sober, but the rest of them are rotten drunk."

"That's in our favor," said Ira.

"I wish Hawkeye was rotten drunk, too," said Cricket. "Sober, he'll be dangerous. But I know how to take him out of the picture."

"How?"

Cricket was suddenly occupied with his saddle rigging. "Just leave it to me."

"Old Paiute way?"

"Right," said Cricket, holding up the powerful short bow and a handful of arrows in a thin quiver. "His friends won't know what hit him."

They tied their horses to two gnarled bitterbrushes that could absorb a horse's lunging. Then, bent nearly double and keeping to the shadows, they made their way toward the cabin that housed the rustlers.

The front gate to the ranch was wide open. "Gate open. Nobody on guard," Cricket whispered. "They're sure of themselves." He raised up and pointed to a small corral next to the ranch house.

"I'll cover you from here, but for Christ's sake, take it slow and quiet."

Ira inched his way to the little corral. The voices from inside the rustlers' cabin were loud enough for him to chance talking to the horse in low tones. "Ayrab," he said. "It's me. You remember me. I used to rub you down every day."

When he felt he could wait no longer, Ira opened the corral gate, stopped when a hinge squeaked, slipped through the aperture, and stood exposed for Ayrab to see him and make up his mind. Ayrab nickered in recognition. Ira crossed the intervening space and put out his hand to touch Ayrab's silken muzzle. Ayrab received the touch, and Ira repeated it, stroking his head and neck in the way he had done at the Hamilton ranch. When he knew the time was right, Ira slipped a noose gently over Ayrab's neck, twisted it into a rough halter, and began leading him toward the gate.

"What the hell!" The hoarse exclamation came on the heels of a clatter of boots on the wooden porch. Ira wheeled and saw Hawkeye's figure outlined against the light from an opened door. Dropping Ayrab's lead rope, Ira raised the Winchester rifle and pointed it blindly at Hawkeye's figure. Certain that he was too late, Ira stiffened in anticipation of Hawkeye's bullets tearing into him.

Instead, he heard the humming of a bow string and the *thunk* of an arrow striking bone. Hawkeye's erect figure folded moaning onto the wooden porch.

"Let's go," Cricket whispered almost in Ira's ear. Without regard for noise, they sprinted for the ranch gate they had come through only minutes before. They were under cover of darkness when the first alarm was sounded from the rustlers' cabin.

"Hawkeye's been hit!"

"You're crazy! There's been no shooting."

"Well, look at him. He's bleeding."

"I'll be double damned. He's got an arrow in him."

After the first week, Ira and Cricket were sure they were not being followed. They had stopped briefly at Marcelino's sheep ranch and told him what happened. He laughed aloud at the way the situation had turned itself around. "You stole him back! You really stole a horse back from a rustler! Wonderful."

Marcelino doubted, too, that Hawkeye would follow Ira and Cricket, especially when Cricket revealed to him what damage an arrow could do. "If he don't die off, he'll be digging obsidian splinters out of his hide for a month," Cricket said gleefully.

"Well, then, let's head for home," said Ira.

"Your home or my home?" said Cricket.

"You decide," said Ira.

14

Every night for twenty-five days, Ira went to the lodge of Black Rock Tom and his wife, Sage Flower, and kneeling at the feet of Thoma, their daughter, went through the ritual of acceptance. When the time was done, he would, according to custom, take her by the left hand and pledge his devotion and join her clan in a wedding feast.

Exchanging the vows was well along, and it was time to talk about the reciprocal visit to the homestead of John D. Hamilton. Ira whistled when the subject came up. "I can't promise anything, Chief. He's my father and I must honor him, but you know he's a stubborn man."

"But you are his son, and he must honor you in his turn," said Black Rock Tom.

It was Cricket's turn to whistle. He had been privy to John

D. Hamilton's sentiments about Indians. "All I can say is 'good luck.'"

"He'll change his mind once he's seen and talked to Thoma," said Black Rock Tom.

"I think so, too," said Ira. "He is partial to pretty women, and Thoma is beautiful."

"Pretty! Beautiful!" mocked Black Rock Tom's wife. "You talk foolishness. That will not change John D. Hamilton's mind. You are forgetting the most important thing of all— Thoma is carrying the seed of Hamilton's line. That makes the difference in his accepting this marriage."

Black Rock Tom nodded, impressed by his wife's wisdom. Cricket shook his head in disagreement. "Or rejecting this marriage," he muttered.

Caught off guard by the open voicing of his and Thoma's lovemaking, Ira flushed and said nothing. He was preoccupied with the unavoidable confrontation with his father, and his remorse for not having the decency to tell his father until the ceremony would be consummated. He felt that he was treating his father shabbily, but with the marriage ceremony only days away, it was too late to do anything about it. He would simply have to suffer the guilt of hurting a man who had not earned hurt.

15

Until now, the only time John D. Hamilton by God had known loneliness was when his wife, Sarah, had died in childbirth. For four years he had suffered in a solitude broken only by visits to the Paiutes' nomadic camps. Ira's precarious infant years were spent at the breast of Black Rock Tom's wife, Sage Flower. It had been a period of mixed emotions for John D. Hamilton, who at once regretted his child having to suckle at an Indian breast, but realizing that if it were not for Sage Flower, Ira Hamilton would certainly have died from malnourishment.

When Ira Hamilton was old enough to be held in front of his father on the saddle, and when he could take mashed rice and potatoes from John D.'s hand, he was returned to the Hamilton ranch. Sage Flower had read John D.'s torment and was more amused than resentful of it. Living with Black

Rock Tom had prepared her for the eccentricities of putting up with John D. Hamilton, who was like her husband in many ways.

When it came time to return Ira to the doubtful nursing skills of his father, she had simply exercised patience, teaching John D. how to prepare mashed oats and cereals and, later, potatoes and minced meats. Milk for the boy had seemed an insurmountable problem until Sage Flower had brought a goat to the Hamilton homestead and taught John D. how to milk it.

By the time Ira had reached the age of twelve, he was not only companion but invaluable helper to John D. Hamilton by God. The only times they were separated were the brief periods when Ira was required to attend classes with students in the Heavenly Valley School, a one-room affair that held only enough classes to fulfill the California school requirement. The rest of his time was spent working stock and helping John D. with the unceasing labor of ranch work. Early on, he had demonstrated a gift for breaking broncos that even John D. Hamilton had qualms about riding. Full-dress rodeos being distant from Hamilton country, Ira's exploits went little noticed until they competed in the Fourth of July rodeo in Heavenly Valley.

Then Ira had set out on his own to reclaim his horse and even his score with Hawkeye, and for the second time in his life, John D. was left to live in loneliness.

Despite his unspoken promise to Ira not to interfere in his personal quest, John D. Hamilton had early on made up his mind to track down his son. Then had come an emissary from Black Rock Tom with the message that Ira, on the trail of the rustlers, had been shot in the back, had been treated by Black Rock Tom's shaman, and was being nursed back to health by the chief's own family. It took the full measure of his considerable stubbornness for John D. to remain at the ranch and not follow the emissary immediately to his wounded son. Only the assurance that Sage Flower was helping to care for Ira forestalled him.

Three months had come and gone without another word from Black Rock Tom. John D. Hamilton had nearly reached the end of his rope. He had to surmise that Ira had either died of his wounds or had gone off on his own to track down the rustlers. Then he remembered that Cricket would certainly be with Ira wherever he went, and that Black Rock Tom would have a good idea of their destination.

John D. had decided to abandon discretion and ride out on the morrow to find Black Rock Tom's gathering, which for near certain had to be at Black Rock Springs.

His first words to himself had been slowly, but irrevocably growing. John D. Hamilton by God was not a man given to examining himself. "It's time," John D. Hamilton said aloud, "to be honest."

He asked himself why he hated Indians, and answered as if by rote, *Because they're no damned good. No that isn't honest.* John D. had known Indians for as long as he could remember. Sure, there had been renegades along the way, but by and large, they were hardworking, clean, and quiet enough to satisfy anyone. John D.'s thoughts carried him further into forbidden ground. He had to admit that Black Rock Tom was a good chief and father. *Do I really hate him?* No, of course he didn't, he had to admit. Neither Tom nor Sage Flower, who had come to John D. in his time of need for his infant son. *Nor Cricket, who is like a brother to Ira.*

But if you don't hate them, then that makes a dishonest man out of you, he thought with a pang of guilt. He asked himself what was the reason he went about talking badly about Indians. Because it was the thing to do in Heavenly Valley.

It was a collective wisdom that was a lie from the beginning, he decided.

Heavenly Valley didn't like Indians. That was for sure. John D. remembered that only ten years before, an eccentric old rancher had been found killed and the town in righteous howling for revenge, had organized not only one posse, but two, to find the Indians who had committed the killings. One posse came back with the news that they had found a Mexican's hoof tracks, which were from a shod horse, who had thrown a Mexican horseshoe. Obviously, he was the murderer. The other posse returned, a little shamefaced but not owning up to it. They had found four Indians camped by the river and killed them all. When they looked around, they discovered the braves were merely hunters shooting meat for a Paiute band. "They were the wrong Indians," they announced without an ounce of guilt bearing them down. John D. said loudly, "They were true murderers, the men who made up that posse." It was the final blow to John D.'s carefully built pillar of righteousness about Indians, and he bowed his head in shame.

The sound of a solitary horse at an unhurried walk broke through John D. Hamilton's examination of conscience. He rose slowly, went to the kitchen door and reached behind it. He found the rifle he kept there for strangers who didn't shout the ranch land hail, "Hello house! Hello house!"

The broad shaft of lantern light from the kitchen stretched out into the yard. John D. Hamilton stepped out of its glare and stood in the shadows with his rifle across his chest. The horse moved unflinchingly into the shaft of light. It was only Cricket. He dismounted and went to John D. Hamilton with serious demeanor. John D.'s heart constricted in his chest.

"Have you come to tell me my son is dead?"

"No," said Cricket. "I came to take you to your son's wedding. He's going to be married."

The words "Like hell he is!" leaped to John D.'s lips, and died there.

"Ira's going to marry my sister," said Cricket.

There was along silence as John D. Hamilton wavered in indecision. Then he said in a rough voice, "My gear is ready. Let's head out."

16

"Why do your people stay here when you know you're not wanted?" John D. said as they rode along.

"My people were here first," said Cricket in the same conversational tone John D. Hamilton was using.

"That makes no matter," said John D. Hamilton. "We won it from your people by settling it. Our fathers didn't even have to fight for it."

"But my people believe that our gods' land is not to be sold," said Cricket. "It has always belonged to everyone who treats it well."

John D. was not prepared to involve himself with Indian gods, especially with an Indian. He abandoned his questioning and asked instead, "All the short cuts to grass and water we have taken this night. Why haven't your people showed the white man where they are?"

"Because the white man would steal them in some way," said Cricket. "Probably sell the trail to other whites, maybe even say Paiutes can't use them."

John D. Hamilton grunted with the knowledge that the white man would do exactly what Cricket was saying. He fell silent and the night was again quiet. At length, he asked the question that he had wanted to ask from the beginning, risking Cricket's anger. John D. Hamilton was well aware there was a line he could not cross without retribution.

"Son," he said disarmingly. "How do you and your people feel about an Indian girl marrying a white man? I'm thinking you have your pride, too." It was a statement that he would never have asked until this unexpected time of examining himself.

Cricket shrugged. "We don't think anything bad at all," Cricket said. "When two people feel about each other the way Ira and Thoma feel, it would anger the gods not to become married."

The Indian gods had intervened again. "I see and I don't see," John D. said. "Maybe time will change me."

Under ordinary circumstances, every approach to Black Rock Springs when Indians were encamped there would have been manned by a sentry in a rock perch. Tonight was the exception.

All eyes watched below at the huge bonfire blazing in front of Black Rock Tom's lodge overlooking the marriage ceremony.

John D. Hamilton made his way unchallenged toward the black opalized pinnacle looming over lodges and people and fires. Painted braves, beaded women, and shamans in full ceremonial dress were grouped around Ira and Thoma who knelt in front of Black Rock Tom and Sage Flower.

Cricket had faded into the maze of lodges, leaving John

D. Hamilton alone to face what he must see. The rigors of John D.'s passage across the desert were written on his face. Desert dust was cut through with rivulets of sweat. His formidable presence was finally recognized by Black Rock Tom when he reluctantly raised his hand in welcome. John D. Hamilton dismounted, dropped his reins, and let himself be led forward. The throng parted and he found himself facing Ira and Thoma robed in white buckskins.

"You could have done me the courtesy of telling me," John D. said to Ira.

"I thought you would say no and never talk to me again."

"People can change, you know."

"Have you changed, Mr. Hamilton?" said Thoma.

John D. said slowly, "I think so."

Thoma took his hand and placed it on her stomach. "Then our child will have a grandfather after all," said Thoma.

John D.'s eyes widened as he slowly understood all that the word implied.

"Then you will be living with me."

"Yes," said Thoma, "most of the time."

"Well, I don't know what people will say about that," said John D. Hamilton. "But then, I don't really give a damn."

At a signal from Black Rock Tom, Cricket emerged from the darkness with the Arab colt. The little horse had been brushed to a gloss and his silken mane was braided. He handed the reins to Ira, who gave them to Thoma. The colt would be the seal of their marriage.

Thoma took the reins and intoned the ritual thanks. In Paiute and in English, Black Rock Tom made the pronouncement of husband and wife forever joined. Understanding why the pronouncement had also been made in English, Ira bowed in thanks.

"What I have done is not only for you, but for your father," Black Rock Tom said in a voice that had lost some of its strength and gruffness.

Ira turned to watch his father. To his amazement, John D. Hamilton was walking toward Black Rock Tom with his hand open.

Over the heads of the wedding party, the eyes of Black Rock Tom and John D. Hamilton—set in their granite countenances—locked in promise. An old and bitter era had come to an end. It was too much to expect that love would supplant it, but a new kinship between two patriarchs and two people would take its place.